MOONSTONE

BOOK II OF THE MYSTIC STONES SERIES

BY KAYLA CURRY

THE MYSTIC STONES SERIES

Moonstone (Mystic Stones Series #2)

Copyright © 2016 Kayla Curry

Editing by Samantha S. Lafantasie

www.KaylaCurry.com

Paperback ISBN: 978-0-9916684-5-8

Ebook ISBN: 978-0-9916684-6-5

All rights reserved.

This is a work of fiction. Names, characters, places, brands, media, and incidents are either the product of the author's imagination or are used fictitiously. The author acknowledges the trademarked status and trademark owners of various products referenced in this work of fiction, which have been used without permission. The publication/use of these trademarks is not authorized, associated with, or sponsored by the trademark owners.

DEDICATION

For those who were taught to dream big and those who weren't taught to dream big but did anyway.

TABLE OF CONTENTS

PROLOGUE

Before the events of Obsidian, there were other incidents leading up to the virus that took out all satellite technology on February 2, 2020. Psytech had been planning the take-over of technology for years. This love story is a look at what happened before the virus went live. It's a story of good and evil and the path to each. It begins on April 26, 2013—about seven years before the virus is unleashed.

CHAPTER ONE

Dorin

Two busy front desk clerks tried to check-in impatient guests at the upscale hotel where I reserved a room. I stood fourth in line, and the woman second in line caught my eye.

She was a healthy thin with long blond hair pulled into a loose ponytail. She had bright blue eyes and held her head high in confidence as she patiently took in the aesthetic of the lobby. Meanwhile, I enjoyed the aesthetic of her long legs.

Judging from her black skirt and blouse, her line of work was corporate. I'd never found a business woman sexy before, but something about her drew me in. Finally, the man in front of me doing a funny little dance lost his patience and walked toward the bathrooms. That's when I first caught the intoxicating scent of the woman in black. I closed my eyes and let the urge to attack her then and there pass. I inwardly scolded myself for the momentary lapse of control.

Now third in line, I had a limited amount of time to make conversation. As I stepped forward, I hit a wall.

She wore only one piece of jewelry—a ring that would make things difficult—not a wedding ring, but something much more ominous. I felt the force inside pushing me away. She acted unaware of its power over me. Of course, the first woman to pique my interest in America would be wearing a protective ring. My luck was nothing if not bad.

2

"That's quite a unique ring you're wearing," I stated. I had to test the limits.

She looked up at me with her big blue eyes and smiled.

"Thank you, my grandmother gave it to me. She carved it herself from a seashell," the woman replied.

The force grew even stronger after I made my presence known—it strengthened the wall between us. Not because of any fear from her, but because I wanted to taste her blood and the vampire spirit inside the ring knew it. The spirit warned my subconscious mind to stay away, therefore physically pushing me away from her. The fact that I couldn't harm her because of my curse was the only reason I'd gotten so close to her to begin with.

If I wanted to have my way, the ring would have to come off.

The curse was only a small problem. Once she kissed me, she would be mine to take.

The woman finished checking in, and I stepped forward to begin my own check-in. I watched from the corner of my eye as she went to her car to unload her luggage. I timed it right so that we ended up taking the elevator together. She stepped in first, and I followed but stuck to the opposite side so the ring wouldn't noticeably affect me. I made small talk—even though such trivial conversation annoyed me to no end—and it turned out we were going to the same floor.

"So, where are you from?" I asked her.

"New York. I drove down here for a meeting today. I'll probably stay the weekend and then I'm headed to Miami on Monday."

"That's funny. That's where I'm planning on ending up. Well, Miami and the Palm Beach area. I'm taking my time. I don't want to arrive before spring break is over," he replied.

"Exactly why I'm staying the weekend. I want to give the crowd a chance to clear out."

The elevator opened on the third floor, and we stepped out. I let her go first again. We walked down the south hall together, although with a large gap between us. Our rooms turned out to be across the hall from each other.

"Looks like we're neighbors," I said as I fiddled with the door key—I couldn't stand plastic cards in place of a real key, but the world changed and I had to do the same.

"Have a good night," I called.

"You too!" she replied.

Once inside my room, I decided to try out a talent I had recently developed.

X-ray vision wasn't as simple as peering through a wall. It was more like a bat's sonar. Incredible concentration was required, which would end up making me thirstier than I already was, but I needed to know more about her.

The ability consisted of simply hearing the sounds in another room and using the reverberations of those sounds as they bounce off objects to get a picture of what was in the room. It worked better if there were a constant noise—like a television. Luckily, that was the first thing she turned on. The news channel she selected provided the perfect level of sound for me to see everything.

Aila

When I closed the door to my room, little butterflies fluttered in my stomach. My neighbor was good looking and had a sexy accent to boot. The dialect was one I couldn't quite place, something out of Europe, most likely South Eastern Europe. I shrugged.

Refocusing myself, I turned on the television to CSNBC and began to unpack. I filled the drawers and hung my important blouses and skirts.

"Now to make adjustments," I said to myself as I walked to the alarm clock and set it for seven. Then I turned my attention to the thermostat. It was a touchy touch screen, but eventually I found my nails did the trick. I liked the temperature to be precisely seventy degrees.

I took out my laptop and set it up on the desk. It waited for the moment I needed to do reports. Working on the weekend wasn't required, but I had work to do before my vacation started the following week. My cell phone charger hung from my suitcase. I plucked the cord out and set it on the endtable.

I grabbed my toiletries then headed for the bathroom. The contents of my makeup bag fit perfectly on the counter. Next, I removed my hair brush from the bag and placed it on the counter for easy access in the morning.

The ice bucket was ready to be filled, so I grabbed it and headed to the hallway. Once I opened my door, I was surprised to see the good-looking man also emerging from his room.

"Well, hello," he said, "I wonder if you could possibly help me. I was just on my way to the desk. The thermostat in my room seems to be either very sensitive or perhaps even broken. I know you don't work here, but personally, I think it's me. Perhaps someone with a better grip on American technology can help."

"Oh, yes. I think I could help you with that. I was adjusting mine and I found that fingernails make the perfect tool," I replied.

He chuckled and glanced down at his well-groomed nails. "That would explain it. I have none to speak of," he said waving his fingers. "Would you mind setting it for me?"

I hesitated. I wasn't sure about going into a strange man's room, but the pocket knife in my jacket reminded me I could take care of myself. I smiled and agreed to help him. He opened his door wider to let me in. His room mirrored mine. I found the thermostat and started toying with it.

"What would you like it set on?" I asked.

"Oh, about seventy, I'd say," he replied.

"That's funny," I said as the thermostat beeped at me, "That's exactly how I set mine."

He chuckled again. "What a coincidence."

"Well, I should get going. I was headed to the ice machine," I said with a smile.

"Of course, don't let me keep you. I'll walk you out," he replied.

I walked into the hallway and glanced back at him. He smiled at me and said, "By the way, my name is Dorin."

"I'm Aila."

"Thank you for your help, Aila. Would you like to join me for dinner at the steakhouse across the street—as a thank you for helping me out with my troubles?" he asked with a charming smile and hope in his eyes.

My confidence broke and I averted my gaze. I thought I might melt if I kept looking at him. I took a second to think it through.

"That would be nice. I was planning on going there anyway. What time would you like to go?"

"Around seven?" he asked.

"Great, I'll see you at seven."

"I'll pick you up," he chuckled. His laugh sent tingles through my stomach.

CHAPTER TWO

Dorin

Aila laughed and waved as she walked toward the ice machine. I took pleasure in seeing my charm at work after all these years. The damn curse wouldn't get in the way. She would be like butter in my hands. American women were suckers for my foreign accent and European charm.

I closed the door and began to prepare for our date—my first date in over a hundred years. I glanced in the mirror and reassured myself that I still had it. I'd lay on the charm nice and thick at dinner and she would eat it up. Then, I'd eat her up. The thought forced a chuckle from my throat.

At precisely seven o'clock, I walked across the hall and knocked on Aila's door. She answered in a timely fashion and her change of clothes nearly knocked me off my feet. I decided right then I would enjoy another kind of pleasure with her before drinking her blood if given the chance.

She wore a little black dress with a touch of blood-red lace hinting at its presence just under the hem and around the neckline. Her heels matched the same deep red color, and her long, curly, golden hair now flowed free from the ponytail she previously wore. Her make-up seemed subtly more dramatic, yet still classy.

"You look exquisite," I said to her. Her heart beat a little faster.

"Thank you," she replied, "You aren't so bad yourself."

We talked about her work and New York on the short walk to the restaurant. I displayed the techniques of a perfect gentleman by opening the door for her and pulling out her chair.

"I'm sorry, but I can't quite place your accent. Where are you from originally?" she asked.

"I'm from Romania. I'm visiting America to see my brother. He moved here a few years ago. I've been here before, but that was a long time ago. I arrived in New York two days ago," I replied.

"How exciting. I've never met anyone from Romania before. I can't say I'm very knowledgeable about that area of Europe. What's it like?" she asked.

"It's beautiful—everything is still half-way stuck in the past. We are a modern yet old-fashioned country. I think you'd like it."

"I'm sure I would. I travel to Europe every now and then for work. I'd love to visit Romania. Isn't that where the legendary novel, Dracula takes place? Or is that Transylvania?" Aila asked.

Dorin chuckled, "Well, actually, it's in Romania, but when Bram Stoker wrote Dracula, the locale for his novel was called Transylvania. Modern day Transylvania is located inside our borders, and the area is still called Transylvania. It's confusing, I know, but it's home."

"That's interesting. People always seem to think Transylvania is a country, but it's actually a region of Romania? I'll remember that."

"The unification of Transylvania and Romania is celebrated annually on the day called Unification Day," I explained.

"Where did you learn to speak English so well?" Aila asked.

"Well, in school we learned French. After I graduated, I took English lessons because my brother was planning to move here and I hoped to one day make the move as well. I love Romania, but American culture is interesting to me. I'd like to have a home in both countries, and spend summers in Romania and the rest of the year here. I own a vineyard, so I would be there for the harvest season, but I could come back for the rest of the time."

"A vineyard? So you must know your wine," Aila said.

"Yes, in fact, I've already ordered us a fine bottle of red I believe you'll love. It's on its way out right now," I said as the waiter emerged from the back with a bottle and two glasses.

"I didn't even notice you order it," Aila said with excited surprise. Her face lit up with satisfaction.

I smiled at her and enjoyed my own excitement. If everything went to plan, I would drink the wine as it coursed through her bloodstream.

"I called ahead after I asked you to dinner. I thought it might be a jovial surprise."

"You didn't need to do that," Aila replied. She ordered a chicken dish and I ordered a steak. Our salads arrived shortly after and conversation was effortless.

As the meal went on, I found that Aila was intelligent and I actually enjoyed her company. Of course, the only thing I had to compare it with was the company of the prostitutes I'd preyed on recently. She grabbed her wine glass and I instinctively glanced down at her hand. She'd taken off her ring. I couldn't believe I hadn't noticed sooner.

At first, my adrenaline surged as it normally did when I was ready to attack. Then a moment of panic hit me. For a split-second, I wasn't sure I wanted to drink her blood anymore.

I immediately pushed the thought out of my head—drinking her blood was the whole point of the night. It didn't matter how intelligent she was or how pleasant her company was—I had been craving something besides a prostitute's disease-tainted blood, and I was going to have it. I deserved something more elegant, which is why I laid on the charm so thickly. She would be mine tonight, and when I finished, I'd move on to my next meal whether she survived or not.

"This is wonderful wine. I've got to hand it to you. You certainly know your business. I'll bet your own wine is even better," she said.

The words snapped me from my obsessive thoughts.

"Well, I don't want to brag, but unfortunately, I didn't think to bring any with me. Although, I believe my brother has some I shipped to him last year in Miami," I replied.

"I'd love to taste it. If you aren't too busy, maybe when we're both in Miami we could get together and you can show me what Romanian wine tastes like."

"Of course. I can make time for you. You'll have to try my tuiça as well," I said. I flashed my charming smile.

I contemplated Aila meeting my brother.

No.

That would not happen. He'd surely try to take her for himself.

My brother shared my curse, but he would not hesitate to try to find a way around it. Perhaps he'd spill her blood first and drink it second-hand. I'd thought of doing that, but blood didn't taste as good if it wasn't straight from the source. I wouldn't allow Andrei to spoil my prize.

"Tuiça? What is that?"

"It's plum brandy. Romania is the world's second largest plum producer—after the U.S. We have to find something to do with all those plums, so we turn them into plum brandy. We call it tuiça."

"Interesting. I'd like to know more about your country. It sounds like a beautiful and peaceful place to live."

"It is, Aila. I'm lucky to have been born in such a magnificent place," I replied. Our food arrived while the conversation continued. The wine and food complemented each other nicely. The meal was cooked to perfection.

My curiosity got the better of me.

"What happened to your ring?" I asked.

"Oh, I must have left it in my room. I took it off to put my lotion on. I usually never forget it. My grandmother gave it to me when I was young. She had to enlarge it a few times to fit me as I grew. She passed away a few years ago and I never travel without it."

"Well, it's quite a remarkable ring. I believe the methods used to carve those are ancient. I've only seen a few others like it. Did she ever tell you what it means?"

"No. She just said it would protect me, even when I didn't know I was in danger. She used to tell me it would keep the monsters away," Aila replied.

I nodded. "Yes, I've heard stories that sailors would wear them to protect themselves from sea monsters. They've been in use for many years."

"Are you a historian as well?"

I chuckled. "Only in my free time. I'd say my interest in history is more a hobby than a career."

The rest of dinner went smoothly and Aila walked close to me in the cool air when we crossed the street back to the hotel. Her close proximity felt strange to me. It was something I hadn't experienced in over a hundred years. I wondered if I should put my arm around her and pull her in closer. She turned her gaze to me and commented on the chilly air. A gentleman would offer his coat, but I wore none so I decided to keep up with the romantic theme of the night and put my arm around her.

"You're cold." She responded to my touch, but not in a way that made me pull my arm back. She said it as if she wanted to warm me.

"I like the cold," I replied, "It makes warmth more enjoyable."

Aila

I laughed gently. The night had been wonderful. I wondered if he were having a good time too. I also wondered if he was this attentive with other women. His charm almost overpowered me. Perhaps it was the fact that he was a foreigner, or maybe it was his exotic good looks with pale skin and dark hair. Add his rugged whiskers that peppered his face and his strong arm around me in the cold night and I was under his spell.

Once we were inside the lobby of the hotel, regrettably, he removed his arm from around me. We entered the elevator together. Fear of what would happen once we reached the third floor brought internal panic.

We were in a hotel.

If I wanted to know for sure that he wasn't looking for a one-night stand, I'd have to get into my room alone. The situation could make things awkward, but I didn't have much to lose. I'd only known him for a few hours.

I'd dodge a night-cap and see how he acted the next day. That would let me decide what he really wanted from me. I wasn't about to have a one-night stand with someone I just met.

The elevator stopped and my heart fluttered. Dorin gestured for me to step off first. The short walk to our rooms was silent, but the smiles on both our faces spoke for us. Like a true gentleman, he didn't try to lead me to his door.

Dorin walked me to my room and stood in the entryway just outside.

I didn't reach for my key right away. Instead, I turned to him and sighed.

"I had a wonderful time tonight. Thank you for dinner and for the wine. And, most of all, thank you for the conversation. I hope I didn't bore you."

"Quite the contrary, I was enraptured by your presence. Your company was more than I could have asked for and I'd like to spend more time with you," he replied with a charming smile.

I wasn't sure if he meant the next day or that moment, but I wanted to take it slow if the connection were to go any further.

"I'd like to spend more time with you too. I do need to tell you, though, that I've just been, well—pushed around by men lately. I want to take things slowly if we decide to further our connection. I hope you can understand that."

"Of course," Dorin said with a hint of disappointment.

I'd killed the mood with my "take it slow" speech, so I settled for kissing him on the cheek before finding my room key and saying good-night.

CHAPTER THREE

Dorin

"Good night," I said. The disappointment hidden behind the façade of my charming smile made me sick.

Once she was safely inside her room, I turned to my door and let myself in. No longer having to be charming, I felt the need to yell and scream. My emotions overcame me like a two-year-old throwing a tantrum.

I was surprised at myself. Up until now, I'd been an emotionless shell. Now the only thing I could think was if only her kiss were two inches to the left, I would have had her. The kiss must be on my lips for my fangs to be released. My disappointment grew because I was sure that tomorrow, even if I did get a kiss, she'd be wearing the ring.

"Damn that useless thing," I said aloud. I was thirsty and now I'd have to settle for a prostitute. It had been days since my last proper meal. The wine at dinner had at least kept me a gentleman, and I might have another chance at Aila if I still wanted it in the morning. I remembered the days I didn't have to be a gentleman to drink blood such as hers. The days I would simply take what I wanted—whom I wanted. Even royalty landed on the menu every now and then.

My brother and I were ruthless, although our ways had gotten us cursed. The fact that we'd kept it a secret from the humans around us was something to be admired.

I sighed before leaving my room to track down a suitable prostitute. Whether or not there could ever be a "suitable prostitute" was up for debate in my mind.

I would need to find a way to get the ring off Aila. I had to be cunning, and the challenge could become half the fun. All I had to do was put my mind to it and I'd trick the ring off her and have her falling for me with ease. My next meal had the dual purpose of giving me the energy I needed to plot and plan my way into a proper meal. One that didn't taste of disease and drugs.

Aila

I entered my room with butterflies in my stomach and a breath in my lungs I could not let out without squealing. I liked him.

He was a gentleman, and he seemed to respect that I wanted to take things slow. I hoped I would see him again the next day.

I remembered the work I was planning to do over the weekend. I decided to get a head start and generate the reports I needed before going to bed, but I kept finding myself stalled with a smile on my face. He'd stolen my focus.

The next morning, I woke to find a dozen red roses outside my door. The note read:

Aila,

Thank you for your company during dinner last night, I hope you will join me again tonight. If you will, please leave a note with the front desk. I know you must have some work to do, so I hope you have a beautiful day.

Pe curănd,

Dorin

The roses smelled wonderful, and the note was handwritten. I wondered what "Pe curănd" meant, so I took out my phone and searched for a translator. I knew it was most likely Romanian.

The translator eventually came back saying it meant 'See you soon.' I smiled as I gathered up my things for work and went out to the hallway. I hoped to see Dorin so I could accept his invitation in person, but he was nowhere to be seen. I rushed to the elevator thinking I might catch him at breakfast, but the breakfast area was close to empty and Dorin was not one of the patrons.

I ate my breakfast with my mind on him. I reasoned that he must be gone for the day, which is why he asked me to leave a note with the front desk. My daydreaming came to a stop as I realized I didn't really have anything to wear for our date tonight. A little shopping before work wouldn't hurt anything.

Before leaving, I stopped at the desk and asked for a piece of paper. The clerk handed me a scribbled on, torn up scrap.

"Do you have anything more—formal?" I asked.

The clerk smiled and gave me a 5X7 sheet of clean white paper.

"Thank you," I said as I wrote my acceptance on the paper.

Dorin,

I would love to eat dinner with you again. I'll be ready at the same time as last night. Thank you so much for the beautiful flowers. They made my day.

Pe curănd!

Aila

I smiled as I handed the paper back to the clerk and asked her to make sure Dorin received it. The clerk promised she would either catch him on his way in or deliver it to his room before she left. Apparently, she was the one who had delivered the flowers as well. I blushed when I learned that a hotel clerk was witness to my blossoming connection to Dorin. I thanked the girl at the desk before going shopping, although I knew the day would drag on slowly since I was excited to see Dorin.

CHAPTER FOUR

Dorin

I entered the hotel after a long day of planning the perfect night. I'd been sure that Aila would accept my invitation and my notions were confirmed upon looking at the face of the front desk girl who'd helped me deliver the flowers. She was excited to see me, which meant she probably had good news. "Mr. Dimir!" she said, "I have a note for you!"

"Yes, thank you." I read the note in front of the clerk, she acted anxious to see if Ms. Myles had accepted, but I had a sneaking suspicion she already knew what the note said. Aila had used my Romanian phrase. She must have looked it up, which impressed me.

I smiled at the clerk and said, "She has accepted. Please send chocolates to her room from me. You can put those on my room as well?"

"Of course, they will be there before she returns from her errands. Is there anything else?" the clerk asked as she locked her green eyes on mine.

I detected a hint of envy in her, but I also detected she was a fan of love and chivalry. I contemplated whether or not I should try to have her blood as well, before deciding against it. She'd been helpful, which was enough for me to leave her alone. Besides, she didn't smell as good as Aila did.

"One last thing," I said.

"Of course," she replied eagerly.

"Could you put her room on mine as well? I'd like to pay for it."

"Uh, sure," the clerk said in a surprised voice, "I'll have it on your receipt when you check out. Will that be all three nights?"

"Yes, please," I said.

"Thank you, and have a nice day," I added before walking to the elevator.

I wasn't sure why I decided to pay for Aila's room. The idea came to my head and went to my voice before I could fully process it. Perhaps it was the fact that she'd thought enough to translate my Romanian phrase, or maybe it was her sexy handwriting. Either way, my attraction to her was growing alarmingly fast and I could feel myself starting to become sentimental. I shook the thought from my head and convinced myself I was just happy to have a decent meal.

Aila

I returned to the hotel after finding the perfect dress. I was anxious to get to my room and prepare for my dinner date with Dorin. The front desk clerk wasn't the same one from this morning, but rather one of the young men who had checked me in the night before. He offered a friendly "Hello," and I replied in the same manner. Once I entered the third-floor hallway, I looked around for Dorin. To my disappointment, the hall remained empty.

In my room, I found chocolates and smiled like a young school girl with a crush. I helped myself to two of them before getting ready. The navy blue dress I bought displayed the perfect shade to bring out my eyes. I found my off-white heels and my pearls accented the dress. I didn't know where we were going, but I was sure it would be somewhere, at least, semi-formal if his actions from the night before were any indicator.

At seven, I heard the much-anticipated knock on my door. My stomach fluttered with excitement. I reminded myself to make sure I wore the ring that captured his attention before. The ring also complemented my pearls. I answered the door to a good-looking man in a gray suit. Dorin seemed just as excited to see me as I was to see him, and of course, I couldn't get enough of that sexy accent.

"Did you receive the chocolates?" Dorin asked.

I smiled and replied, "I've already had some of them, thank you."

"I hope you didn't ruin your dinner, we're going to a little place with a large selection of good food, or so I'm told by the front desk clerk."

"Don't worry, I'm definitely ready for some real food," I said.

"Me too," Dorin replied with a sly grin. He led me down the hallway and into the elevator as we slipped into small talk.

CHAPTER FIVE

Dorin

She was wearing the ring.

She held out her hand for me to take.

I didn't want to seem like I was afraid, so I sent out a silent signal to the vampire spirit inside that my curse meant I could not hurt the wearer of the ring unless she kissed me on her own free will. It seemed to work. The ring let-up slightly and I held her hand with some effort. I wouldn't be able to kiss her even if she wanted to while she was wearing that ring. If I did manage to do so, I'd be forced away from her with a burst of energy from the ring, but if everything went to plan, the ring wouldn't be an issue.

I hired a car service that came highly recommended among my kind. Waiting under the awning was a classy black vehicle driven by a relatively new vampire named Bill. Bill opened the door for us as we approached. The drive wasn't long, but I hadn't bothered to learn the driving laws of the United States and I wanted to focus on Aila.

The exclusive restaurant burst at the seams with conversation from rich and overindulgent patrons. I'd paid a lot of money to get short notice reservations along with the other surprises I planned for her. We were seated in a private area, where our conversation took off and was interrupted only momentarily by the delivery of the wine I pre-ordered and the taking of our food order, but we easily started up again.

"So, you said you've been to the U.S. before. When was that?"

"Oh, years ago, when I was about twenty. My brother and I came here to visit a friend of ours. Soon after our return my brother, Andrei, decided to come back here and start a sugarcane plantation. I stayed in Romania to run the vineyard. Together we could make so much happen, which is why I'm here now."

"So you're looking to expand and possibly merge?" Aila asked curiously.

"Yes. I believe my brother and I should work together and make something more. We're already doing well apart, but together we could do even better," I answered.

"You must be close. You speak highly of him," Aila said gently.

"Yes, but it seems the distance over the past years has pushed us apart. I only hope it's not too late to become close again."

"Blood doesn't turn to water," Aila replied.

The words caught me off guard. My mother used to say the same thing in my native tongue, *"Sângele, apa nu se face."* She would say it when Andrei and I would fight with each other. Aila brought something from my childhood out. Something I'd long forgotten.

"My mother used to say that," I commented. "It's quite a popular saying in Romania," I added with a smile.

"Really? My mother used to say it too. She'd say it when my aunts and uncles would fight. She was the peacekeeper in the family. How do you say it in Romanian?" Aila asked.

"Săngele, apa nu se face," I replied with a smile. "That reminds me. I was impressed to see you looked up the phrase in my note. Most wouldn't go through the trouble."

"Well, I was curious and I'm always eager to learn. I suppose my inner nerd showed itself today."

I never heard the word "nerd" before. "Don't laugh, but what is a nerd? My English is pretty good, but there are still some words I don't know."

Aila tried not to laugh, but my smile made her giggle and blush a little before answering.

"A nerd is someone who likes to study the things others would think boring. Someone who likes to do research and be overly organized."

"Well, that doesn't sound so bad. In fact, it might be perfect for the event I have planned for after dinner if you'd like to accompany me."

"What event are we talking about?" Aila asked.

I smiled. "Well, I rented out the Science Museum of Virginia for the night. I thought you might like to join me."

Aila gulped. "You rented it out? You didn't have to go through all that trouble. We could have just gone with everyone else visiting the museum," Aila said with a smile.

"Well, they were going to be closed for the evening, so I asked them how much it would cost to get the two of us a private tour after hours," I replied.

"I don't know if you're charming or just crazy, but yes, I would love to go with you to the museum after dinner."

"Wonderful. I think we'll have a lot of fun. They have a nice collection of interactive exhibits. There's one, in particular, I'm looking forward to."

The excitement was plain as day on Aila's face, which made me start to feel something I hadn't felt in a long time. Such a long time, in fact, that I wasn't sure what the emotion was. Happiness? Fondness? Perhaps my own excitement?

No.

I was excited about the possibility of finally having access to her blood, not about seeing her happy. My own happiness could only be a result of the anticipation I felt about that ring coming off.

Dinner ended, and then I led Aila to the waiting car. Bill promptly drove us to the museum. Inside, four staff members awaited our arrival. They welcomed us with warm, friendly faces and led us past the Foucault Pendulum. We entered the planetarium where we explored the solar system, and then we visited a static electricity exhibit where we each took pleasure in seeing each other's hair stand on end. After a few laughs, we headed to the EcoLab exhibit.

The EcoLab provided each of us with a sample of water with leaves and debris inside. The goal was to find small invertebrates amongst the debris and examine them under a microscope.

"These kinds of experiments have always been fun and interesting in my book," Aila said.

"Do you want me to put your ring in my pocket so you don't lose it?" I asked casually.

"That would be nice, thank you," Aila said. A small pulse of energy burst from the ring but died as soon as she slipped it off her finger and handed it to me. She dove right into the small tub of water and debris. Her eyes searched through the murky water with curiosity. She was unaware of the trouble she'd just invited.

I smiled, although, I wasn't sure if it was because of her excitement or because I'd gotten the ring off. My uncertainty annoyed me.

We ended up finding quite a few little creatures and Aila enjoyed seeing them through the microscope. I didn't need the microscope with my superior vampire vision, but I put on a show. After a few more exhibits, we climbed into the hired car and went back to the hotel.

All I had to do was keep her mind off her ring and on me. I wanted her kiss badly, but it was becoming unclear why I wanted it.

My mind wondered if it was to drink her blood or to satisfy something in me that had been left unsatisfied for so many years.

I shook my head. The conflicting thoughts left me unsettled. I questioned whether or not I could follow through with my plan.

Aila

Dorin's efforts impressed me, but I couldn't help but wonder why he would do such a thing for a woman he just met. I wondered if he did the same thing with other women.

We were headed back to the hotel, so I would have to figure it out soon. I hated myself for the question I was about to ask but promised myself that if the answer satisfied me, I'd find a way to bring back the romantic mood of the evening.

"Dorin," I began, "Why did you go to such lengths to impress me tonight?"

He was obviously caught off guard by the question. He paused to reposition himself in the seat to that he could see me better. He cleared his throat, looked me in the eyes, and answered.

"Honestly, something about you draws me in—makes me want to see you smile. You're so different than Romanian women—and American women for that matter. I can't explain my attraction, it's just—*Ai aprins flacarea in inima mea*—you've lighted up the fire in my heart."

I couldn't believe the words that fell from his perfect lips. The perfect answer.

The fact that I doubted him made me banish the paranoia I'd been fighting. I did the only thing I could think of to make up for my silly inquiry. In the backseat of the hired car, with the privacy window up, I kissed him.

He kissed me back with a warm passion I desired more than anything.

CHAPTER SIX

Dorin

The words left my throat on their own, but they brought out only the truth. She changed something in me—brought out the man I was before I was forged into a weapon—a creature of the night.

And without warning, Aila kissed me. It was something I wanted since I first met her, but I could never have prepared for the passion with which she kissed me—or the way I kissed her back.

I realized I wanted her in more ways than one. I wanted her touch, her happiness, her love—and her blood. But I couldn't have it both ways.

Her blood was now mine to take, but I dared not take it and end the one good thing that had happened since my awakening, or even before that—since my induction into the hell that was immortality. I wasn't sure if I should ever indulge in her blood. If I tried to drink from her, I didn't know if I could stop. Even if I did, she would never want me near her again. She had no idea what kind of monster I was.

The words "curse breaker" flowed like water into my already full mind. I pushed them away. They gave me too much hope, but my mind wouldn't be silenced.

I always believed I would be the one chosen by the woman to break the curse, not my brother. I never expected it to happen so soon, though. We'd only been awake for a few years after our first hundred-year slumber. I stopped kissing Aila and looked deep into her eyes. I didn't know what to do. I needed room to think.

As if she could read my mind, she said, "Let's drink some more wine. My treat this time."

"Only if I get to choose the bottle," I replied with a grin.

"As you wish, Mr. Great Wine Connoisseur." She grinned back at me. "Where should we drink it?"

"Wherever you want," I replied.

Dear God, I was hers. The control I'd held migrated to her hands. This was not how the night was supposed to go. She was supposed to be under my spell, not the other way around.

"How about the rotunda? I'm sure it's quite empty this time of night."

"That sounds wonderful. It's a beautiful night," I replied. I was thankful she'd chosen somewhere private but not too private. I needed to figure out what I was going to do with her.

We entered the lobby to find the two male front desk clerks. I chose a wine and Aila asked them to put it on her room. I smiled because her room was actually on my tab and she didn't even know.

We went out to the rotunda in the cool spring air to wait for our wine. Aila seemed to be somewhat chilled, so I took off the jacket to my suit and placed it over her shoulders as I stood behind her. We both gazed at the courtyard filled with plants and flowers that lined winding paths.

"You're such a gentleman," she said to my touch.

"It's how I was raised," I replied. My mother popped into my mind again. My right hand slipped into the pocket of my slacks as my left hand rested on the small of Aila's back. I fiddled with the ring, not sure what to do with it. One quick move of my fingers and I could snap the delicate shell in half, but she would be devastated if she ever found out. I sighed and took my hand out of my pocket so as not to draw attention to the fact that her ring was still in my possession.

We made our way to a bench and I put my arm around her. "You're leaving Monday morning, correct?" I asked.

"Yes, and you?"

"I'm also leaving Monday morning. How far are you planning on going?"

"I was thinking about stopping around Jacksonville for the night and having a short drive the next day to Miami. I have a meeting on Wednesday, but my vacation officially starts on Thursday, so I'll take a week off and I'm planning on staying in Miami for most of it."

"I was also thinking about stopping in Jacksonville. I don't like to push my driver too hard. Eight hours is a lot for one man," I replied.

"So, you've hired the driver for the duration of your stay?"

"Yes, I didn't want to mess around with getting an American license so I thought it would be easier that way. If you want to ditch your rental and ride with me you're welcome to do that, although, I must warn you—eight hours in the car with me and you may not find me so charming."

"I don't think I could ever not find you charming," Aila replied with a grin.

A hotel employee came to the rotunda with a cart and delivered the wine and two glasses. I poured the wine and handed a glass to Aila. She sipped and seemed to appreciate the perfect balance of the wine I'd chosen. Her face relaxed and so did her shoulders.

"This is phenomenal red wine," Aila said. Her blue eyes looked at me in the moonlight.

My mind raced. Too many feelings swirled around. I wasn't used to a bombardment of emotions.

I'd worked so hard to be able to taste her blood and now that nothing held me back, I couldn't bring myself to do it. The ball was now in her court—so to speak. If she decided to ride with me to Miami, then I'd put everything on the table. I'd introduce her to Andrei and tell her about the curse and about what I was. If she decided not to ride with me I'd make a clean cut and never see her again.

"It comes from a great winery with a top notch reputation in America. It's comparable to mine in Romania. I wish you could taste my Feteasca Neagra. It has the most beautiful color and only gets better with age. I hope my brother still has a bottle."

"Well, if the offer still stands, I think I would like to ride with you to Miami. I'd like to get to know you better," Aila replied.

Adrenaline spiked. The decision made.

"Of course it still stands. I'd be delighted to have you along with me. You wouldn't have to drive and it will save you money on the car rental. Your company is all I need to make my trip to Miami a pleasant one," I said as I pulled Aila closer to me on the bench.

"I think it will be much better for me too," she replied.

"*Ma saruta, draga mea,*" I said as I kissed her again.

Aila ran her hand long the side of my face and asked, "What did you say? It sounded so beautiful."

"It means, kiss me, my dear—*ma saruta, draga mea.*"

"Your language is so beautiful," Aila said as she placed her head against my chest and stared out toward the garden. We sat for a long while—silent and warm. I was sure she even dozed off for a moment in my arms.

"Aila," I whispered, "I think we should get you to bed."

"I think you're right," she said sleepily.

I led her inside to the elevator and then to her room. I stayed while she found her key and let herself in. The thought crossed my mind that I could take her now. I could walk right through her door with her and drink her warm delicious blood, but I found hesitation.

"Good night," Aila said.

"Noapte bun," I replied as I gave her one more kiss.

She smiled and closed the door as I backed toward my own. She'd be asleep soon. The wine had prolonged my meal from the night before, so I didn't need to find a prostitute. I would need to drink the following night if I were going to keep myself away from Aila during our trip. I sat on my bed and concentrated on the sounds in Aila's room to see that she got safely to bed. All the while I thought about how easily I could break a flimsy hotel door.

Aila

I closed the door to my room and sighed with a giant smile on my face. Dorin was such a gentleman, and so different than the men I dated before. I looked at the clock and quickly began getting ready for bed. I took off my dress and slipped into my pajamas. It was then that I realized I left my ring with Dorin. I contemplated knocking on his door and asking for it, but he was probably tired and maybe even already asleep. I wasn't sure if I wanted him to see me in my pajamas either.

"I'll get it from him tomorrow," I said aloud, and then continued to put on my lotion, brush my teeth and climb into bed. I turned on the television and turned off the bedside lamp. My mind was stuck on Dorin. Everything he'd done. Everything he'd said. Every inch of his perfect body and every detail he'd planned for our perfect date. I slipped off to sleep and into a dream about him.

———

Dorin sat across a table from me in a crowded room. Music and colorful lights dulled my dream senses. Wine barrels were everywhere. Soon, the music stopped and another man entered the room behind Dorin. He looked so much like Dorin that I knew it was Andrei, his brother. Andrei came to our table and sat between us with a mischievous look on his face. Dorin appeared annoyed at his presence but was polite enough to introduce us.

Andrei was just as charming as Dorin, except his demeanor was more condescending, as if he used his charm as a weapon. Eventually, Andrei said something I couldn't hear to Dorin and Dorin immediately attacked him. The two brothers were locked in a punching, rolling brawl and I could do nothing to stop them. I tried to yell at them, but nothing came out.

I woke to the red light of the alarm clock at my bedside. It was three in the morning. I tossed and turned and eventually went back to sleep, but dreamed again of the scene of Dorin and his brother fighting. The rest of the night went the same and I woke at my usual 7 o'clock and slowly began to get ready for the day.

I thought I'd pay a visit to Dorin, but I wasn't sure if he was awake quite yet. After our late night I didn't want to wake him, so I decided to slip a note under his door.

On my way out, I stopped and smelled the roses he sent me the morning before. A smile came to my face as the aroma filled my nose. I pulled myself away from the beautiful arrangement and opened the door only to find another. On the floor, sat a vase of fresh red roses in the same arrangement as the prior morning. I smiled when I looked across the hall to see Dorin standing in the entryway to his door.

"I had to see your face this time," he explained.

I smiled and bent down to pick them up and smell them. "They're just as beautiful as the first ones. Thank you," I said as I closed the distance to give him a kiss. He put his arms around me and pulled me in close to kiss my forehead.

"I have something else for you too. Something I forgot to return to you last night," he said as he brought my ring out of his pocket.

"Oh, thank you. I realized I'd forgotten it last night after I got in, but I didn't want to wake you. Thank you for keeping it safe for me," I said as I slipped it back onto my finger.

"I know how much it means to you," he replied.

I opened the door to my room and put the new flowers next to the old ones. Dorin stood just inside the doorway.

"What are you up to today?" I asked.

"Well, I'm not sure yet. Most of my day will be consumed with thinking of you."

I blushed at the sweet words he always seemed to say.

"What about you?" he asked as I closed the door to my room and the two of us walked toward the elevators.

"I was thinking about doing some sightseeing. It's been awhile since I took a tour of Richmond."

"I know a great place to do some sightseeing. Would you like to have a late lunch with me? The place I have in mind is about an hour away, but from what I hear it's worth the wait."

"I'd love to. It's not too fancy is it?"

Dorin chuckled. "No, nothing too fancy."

"Why do I get the feeling your idea of fancy and my idea of fancy aren't quite the same?" I asked.

Dorin chuckled again with a sly grin. "Is there anything you want to do before we go to lunch? We have some time to kill."

"I was thinking about dropping in on one of my college friends. She moved here after we graduated and I haven't seen her in at least a year. You could come with me if you'd like."

"That's alright. I have a few phone calls to make. Why don't you go see her, enjoy a little girl time, and we'll meet back here around noon?"

I smiled and nodded, "That sounds perfect."

We kissed one last time and I left the hotel and found my rental car in the parking lot.

CHAPTER SEVEN

Dorin

I kissed her once more before seeing her off. I was glad the ring hadn't pushed me away. It would be useful for keeping my brother at a distance. I dreaded introducing Aila to Andrei, but there was no other way. The witch had specified that the woman to break the spell must meet both of us. *One who knows the truth, one who sees skin and tooth. This cycle shall repeat, until love the brothers meet.*

I pulled out my cell phone as I walked back into the hotel. I dialed Andrei's number.

"Hello?" Andrei's voice said on the other end.

"It's me," I replied.

"Ah, little brother. To what do I owe the pleasure of this call? I thought I'd be seeing you in a few days. You are still coming, aren't you?"

"Yes, of course. I wanted to give you a heads up. I'm bringing someone."

"Bringing someone? Someone like us?"

"No, she's not. She's human. She's not going to be staying with us, but I'll be bringing her to dinner on Tuesday."

"A human? At dinner? Is she a snack?" Andrei asked.

I had expected this sort of reaction. I'd have reacted the same way only a few days ago. "No. She's my guest. She's not to be touched and she wears a protective ring."

"Then how are *you* getting near her? Don't tell me you've gone soft. The ring senses no danger in you? That's ridiculous. You're as blood-thirsty as I am."

"I used to be. This one's different."

There was a long pause on Andrei's end, then he started laughing.

Once the laughter subsided enough that he could speak again, he said, "You don't think she's the one, do you? That's why you want me to meet her? So that you can break the curse for yourself and leave me in the dust? You know that's a myth don't you? The woman is a lie the witch made up to give us hope and even if it *is* true, I will not stand by while you take the prize."

"This is not about a competition. This is about not wanting to go back to sleep for another hundred years. You'll be exactly the way you are now—unchanged and the curse will be broken for you as well, no more winning a kiss before you drink the blood of a woman."

"Too bad all the blood in the world will not satisfy me if she chooses you. You are correct in assuming that I do not need anyone by my side, but if you think I'm going to let you be the one who can be free of the curse and still enjoy the finer things in life, you're sorely mistaken."

"You've had your chance. You've been here in America while I've been back home taking care of business and not worrying about finding a woman to break the curse. You've had the last three years to do whatever you wanted over here. It's my turn and I'm not wasting it."

"We'll see, little brother. We'll see who she picks. You know as well as I that she has to meet both of us and she must know everything about us. The fact that you lied to her is going to be your undoing and I will be the one to swoop in and pick up the pieces when she thinks she's been fooled."

My anger mounted. Andrei may be right, but once Aila learned the truth, it may be best for her to run and never look back. I was afraid of her finding out what I was. I hoped she'd understand the fact that I had to keep it a secret if she could get past the fact that I was the villain in the most deranged fairy tale ever told. I had to prepare her somehow—give her some sort of hint.

"You don't know her, Andrei. She's not the typical woman."

"I may not know her, but I will. See you soon little brother. I'm looking forward to our reunion," Andrei said before hanging up the phone.

My anger overflowed and I threw the phone across the room. It left a large dent in the metal air conditioning unit and shattered to pieces. I'd replace it another time. I needed to blow off some steam before my lunch date with Aila. I needed blood, but the thought of a prostitute sickened me in more ways than one. The thought of taking any woman's blood sickened me. Aila was changing me for the better.

"I can't starve myself," I said out loud. I looked at the clock. Time wasn't on my side.

I opened the mini-fridge.

A bag of blood for emergencies only beckoned to me. Cold, bagged blood was unappetizing, but I had no choice. Even more unappetizing—it was the blood of a man. I always thought it was odd that vampires usually craved the blood of the opposite sex and didn't care for blood from their own gender. No matter. It still did the job.

I grabbed it roughly and consumed it in just a few large gulps. The amount was barely enough to calm me, although not as satisfying as warm blood would be, it would do for now.

Aila

I returned to the hotel at noon and found Dorin waiting patiently in the lobby. "Hello!" I said. "I've been thinking about you and where we'll be dining."

He opened his arms for an embrace and I happily obliged.

He held me tight as he kissed me and said, "I've been thinking about you as well, and the place we're going is a surprise. Everything has been arranged, and we'll enjoy a wonderful meal in an exquisite setting. Let's get going."

"You truly are a man of mystery," I replied as we walked out to the car.

The long car ride was filled with laughter and conversation. Finally, we arrived at a large vineyard. There was a sign reading: Barboursville Vineyards and Palladio Restaurant.

"What a beautiful place," I said.

"Yes—almost as beautiful as my vineyard. This will do for now until I can get you to come to Romania with me. We're having lunch at the Palladio. The chef there, I hear, is brilliant. Then after we eat, we'll tour the vineyard," Dorin replied.

Lunch was delicious. We shared an appetizer and ate a first and second course, barely leaving enough room for a wonderful dessert. Wine was served with each course; all produced by the Barboursville Vineyard. Dorin tasted the wine with a critical tongue. He enjoyed it, but nothing compared to his, I assumed. I was anxious to try the wine that Dorin had hand-picked the grapes for and labored for hours over every detail. His attention to detail was one of the reasons I was so attracted to him.

We toured the grounds with only a guide at our side. I learned about Dorin's passion as he whispered facts left out by the guide into my ear. The tour ended with a glass of wine on the patio overlooking the deck, and the two of us left alone to talk about whatever we wanted.

"Thank you for bringing me here. I've learned so much about what you do and why you're so passionate about it. I wish my career focused on one of my passions," I said.

"Why shouldn't it? What are your passions?" Dorin asked as he brought himself closer to me.

"Well, I like to sketch my own interior designs. I love to curl up with a good book. I do some baking—cakes, cookies and pastries."

"So why not be an interior designer or open a bake shop?" Dorin asked.

"I don't know. I guess my family always wanted me to be in the corporate game. My father was after his military career and I suppose I followed in his footsteps. I could do those things, but I guess I just did what I thought I was supposed to do."

"Viaţa asta-i bun pierdut, de n-o trăieşti cum ai fi vrut— Life is a waste if you didn't live as you would have wanted to."

"You're right. I've been doing this so long that if I were to do something new, it may not be with the same amount of efficiency as what I've been doing. I guess I'm just chicken," I replied.

"You aren't a chicken. You don't want to disappoint your parents, but you might end up disappointing yourself if you don't follow your soul."

"No more excuses. Maybe in my free time I'll start putting together a business, or I'll take a few classes on interior design."

"We could look into taking one together during your vacation if you'd like. I've shown you my passion. It's your turn to show me yours."

I smiled and nodded.

"By the way. Did you have reservations at a hotel in Jacksonville? I haven't made mine yet and I thought since we're driving together it may be more convenient to stay at the same hotel," I said.

"Yes, I did. I reserved a room at the Danbury. I know we aren't quite at that stage yet, but if you'd like, you can stay with me. I could change it to a two bedroom suite. If you'd feel more comfortable in your own room, I understand that as well," Dorin replied.

"I wouldn't want you to pay for everything. I would pay for half if we got the two bedroom suite. I'd like to spend time with you, but aren't you afraid of seeing too much of me?"

"What a silly thing to ask. One can never see too much of a beautiful and brilliant woman." Dorin said. Then he added, "Aila, I'm beginning to care deeply for you. I want to find out

42

where this leads. If you feel the same, then just say the word and we can both dive in head first. I realize it won't be easy, but you brought out something in me that has been buried for what seems like a hundred years, and I don't want to let it go."

I thought it over for a moment. My feelings for Dorin were becoming stronger with each minute we spent together.

"I do feel the same. I'm just afraid of getting hurt. I know you don't think you'll ever hurt me, but I'm not ready to go too deep. I'll dive in head first, but for now, I'd like to come up for air before we venture too deep. I think the two bedroom suite would be appropriate, but I'll pay for half."

Dorin smiled. "That all seems reasonable. All except for the part about splitting the bill, but that can be discussed later. Right now I want to enjoy your company on this beautiful day."

The rest of the afternoon was blissful. I felt comfortable in Dorin's company. I couldn't stop myself from thinking about how close, I was to falling in love with him. I didn't know why but I felt drawn to him from the moment we met. I wanted to know everything about him. I had plenty of time to learn more about him, at least until my vacation ended and I had to go back to New York. I didn't want to think about what would happen to our relationship when that happened, but I hoped it would continue.

Close to five o'clock, we decided to head back to the city and loaded back into the car for the drive. We rode in comfortable silence for most of the way, breaking our silence a few times to ask random questions. I lounged in Dorin's arms for the ride and we took pleasure in a glass of wine from the bottle Dorin bought from the vineyard.

"So, what shall we do tonight?" I asked. Only realizing I assumed we'd spend it together after the words left my mouth.

To my relief, he replied, "I was just thinking about that. I wondered if you'd enjoy a quiet night of watching movies and things of that nature. We could order room service or eat at the hotel restaurant. Or we could go to the theater and catch a movie there. Whatever you wish to do is fine with me."

"I'm still pretty full from the lunch we ate. I think a nice quiet night in sounds lovely. We could order some snacks and watch movies. Maybe some hot chocolate?"

Dorin embraced me and whispered in my ear, "Perfect."

CHAPTER EIGHT

Dorin

Once we returned to the hotel, Aila and I ended up in her room to watch movies and eventually order room service. We cuddled on her couch and talked more than we watched, but I didn't care. I just wanted to know her. I needed to learn every detail of her life. We asked each other questions about our favorite things and past experiences. I tried to be as truthful as I could, but I couldn't reveal everything quite yet. I planned to tell her before we arrived in Miami.

At some point, Aila fell asleep on the couch nestled against my chest. The warmth of her breath relaxed me. A dark thought came and went. They were becoming less frequent now, but I was still grateful for the ring on her finger as a security measure.

I debated staying with her through the night, but at lunch she'd made it clear she wasn't quite ready for that, so I gently picked her up and placed her in bed. Before I left, I wrote a note to her and left it on her table. I kissed her forehead before leaving her room for my own.

My thirst returned. My emergency blood had not lasted long and I needed blood before our trip tomorrow. I couldn't make myself hurt another innocent person. The thought of going to the crime-riddled side of town and drinking from someone who deserved to die hit me. But, the taste of a man's fresh blood was unappetizing—at least stale blood in a bag masked the taste a little. The thought of hurting any woman, no matter how horrible a human she was, didn't appeal to me either. This repulsion was new to me. A switch had been flipped. I'd become one of those vampires that break into local blood banks. I flipped open the phone book in my room to search for the nearest Red Cross.

I decided to grab some extra for the trip and the stay in Miami. I couldn't take any chances with Aila by my side.

Aila

I woke to the sound of the alarm clock. Immediately, I looked around for Dorin. My heart fluttered as I turned my head one way and then the other. Disappointment sunk in when I realized he was gone, but then I found the note. My heart pounded again. I couldn't stand the thought of him leaving. As I read the note, I realized I shouldn't have worried.

Aila,

I hope you slept well. I left last night because I knew you weren't ready for me to stay the night quite yet. I wanted to be respectful of your wishes, so I made sure you were comfortable and went to my room. I hope I did the right thing. Today we set off for Jacksonville. Please join me for breakfast if you wish. I know you always wake at seven, so I'll be by at eight to wish you good morning in person.

Dorin

I breathed a sigh of relief. He hadn't left without me. I scolded myself for being so silly.

I couldn't wait to see him again. With excitement as my fuel to get going, I showered, got dressed and put on my make-up in only half an hour. I had my bags packed by the time a knock came at my door, precisely at eight. I rushed to greet Dorin with a smile on my face.

When I opened the door, there he was smiling and leaning on the entrance way wall in the same sexy manner he always did. His dark hair fell to his cheek and his perfect teeth showed through his smile. His brown eyes stared into mine and held them captive.

"Good morning," I managed to say.

Dorin kissed me and whispered, "Good morning, my dear."

"I'm ready for breakfast. Did you want to eat here at the hotel?"

"I hear they're having your favorite breakfast item today—French toast."

"Mm. You remembered. We spoke of that on our second date."

"I remember everything you tell me."

I smiled wider and we went down to breakfast. The French toast was accompanied by eggs and bacon. Soon we returned to our floor to retrieve our things before we got on the road. Dorin loaded everything up for me. I felt like royalty around him. It was too much—he was too much. I'd never get over the way Dorin worked so hard to make sure I was happy and comfortable.

The long drive seemed to bring us closer.

Eight hours with a few breaks, one for lunch and a few others for quick sight-seeing and stretching our legs. We talked about a lot of things on the way. We learned as much about each other as possible. Dorin's descriptions of Romania made me want to move there and never look back. His words dripped with beauty and elements of a time that had long since passed.

CHAPTER NINE

Dorin

I peered down at the sleeping woman in my arms. We neared Jacksonville and I'd soon have to wake her.

I wanted more than anything to be able to tell her everything. The anxiety of Aila not knowing the truth grew with every conversation we had that didn't end in telling her I was a cursed vampire with a dark past—a past not far behind me.

I ran my fingers through her long, wavy, golden hair. A slight smile developed on her face. I wondered what she was dreaming about. I wished I could sleep. I'd dream about her if I could. If I had to sleep for another hundred years I could keep her in my thoughts. I hoped our lives were meant for more. If she wasn't the one to break the curse, no woman was.

We entered Jacksonville city limits into a high traffic area. The change of speed woke Aila. She sat up and looked around, "Jacksonville?"

"Yep. We should be at the hotel soon. What would you like for dinner?"

"Maybe we should see what's near the hotel and decide from there. I think something deep fried sounds good. Have you ever had American fast food?"

"Fast food? Aren't those establishments—questionable?"

"Yeah, I suppose, but KFC is usually pretty good. I'd love some Kentucky Fried Chicken right now . . . with mashed potatoes. Yum."

I laughed, "If you insist. I'll give it a try."

"I do." Aila replied.

Aila

I was satisfied with my KFC, and Dorin didn't seem to mind it either. He ate his chicken to the bone. The wrappers and containers were strewn across the little coffee table in the main room of our suite.

"What did I tell you? Good, huh?" I said with a grin.

"You were right. I guess some fast food in America is okay."

I laughed. I was happy to be the one to introduce him to part of the American "culture." After dinner, we enjoyed some wine and talked. I taught Dorin how to play a few American card games. I won most of them, but I had the suspicion that he let me win at least a few of them.

After a game of Mao, in which I made a rule that we had to kiss whenever a two of hearts was played, we curled up on the couch. Dorin stroked my hair as we watched television and I ran my finger along the lines of his free hand.

"Do you think fate planned our meeting?" I asked.

"If it was, then whoever's in charge of fate has smiled upon me. When I saw you standing there in the lobby, I was immediately enamored by you. Our meeting changed me. I know you don't understand now, but you will."

"What do you mean?"

"For now, all I can say is if I hadn't met you, I'd be lost to a side of me that I'm not proud of," he replied.

I sighed and looked at him. I didn't want to pry because it seemed like something he wasn't ready to share yet, but I wanted to let him know it was safe. "You can tell me, you know. I won't judge you based on your past. I'm the kind of person that cares more about who you are now rather than who you used to be."

"I sense that about you, but the time isn't right. I'll tell you very soon, I promise. Before we meet my brother, you'll know what I'm talking about. Now, let's talk about something more light-hearted, shall we?"

"I have a better idea," I said. I didn't know what came over me, but I wanted to kiss Dorin so badly at that moment—so I did.

He kissed me back passionately. My lips parted and our tongues entwined. I pushed myself toward him and he pulled me into his arms. I sat on his lap with my legs on either side of him as we kissed and let our hands explore each other's body.

I let my lips leave his to get a deep breath and in that time, he started kissing my neck. He took a deep breath through his nose and then stopped. He held my face in front of his and I noticed the look in his eyes. He seemed to be conflicted about something.

"Aila, I want to respect your wishes, we should slow down. You have no idea how bad I want you—in more ways than one, but I can't go any further with you tonight."

I took a deep breath. "You're right."

I dismounted and settled for the cuddling position we'd held earlier. He wrapped his arms around me again and hugged me close to his body.

"I can't seem to get enough of you," Dorin said, "but I want to make sure you're one hundred percent ready before we get too caught up in it all."

I smiled. "You have no idea how much that means to me. I'm lucky to have found a gentleman like you."

We stayed up late and talked until I felt like I'd fall asleep mid-sentence. Dorin led me to my room and gave me a sweet good-night kiss.

CHAPTER TEN

Dorin

I kissed Aila as she retired to her bedroom. I used my ability to make sure she got to bed safely.

For a moment, I remembered kissing her neck. God, it was all I could do to keep from sinking my teeth in. Her ring had even put out a short burst of energy. She didn't notice, but part of me wished she had. If she had questioned that one little pulse, I could have come clean then and there.

I started worrying about how to tell her about everything. I didn't know how she'd take it. I decided it was best to do it at the hotel in case she did decide to leave. Logically, I needed to do it first thing in the morning.

All night I churned words through my head. I came up with an explanation for everything. I'd have an answer for every question she could possibly ask—provided she stuck around.

Soon, the sun began to rise, and although she hadn't set her alarm clock, I knew she'd wake up around seven.

I heard her start to move about in her room and eventually she came out to greet me. She looked beautiful even without her make-up on. Her golden locks tangled in a sexy way. She was naturally beautiful and I hoped I'd be able to admire her beauty for the rest of my long, long life—even if only in photographs.

"Good morning!" she said. She walked toward me to give me a kiss. I opened my arms and kissed her as if it may be our last kiss. Her smile was wide as she came away from me. I'd miss that smile if these were our last moments together.

"Bun dimi neata," I replied in my native tongue.

Aila sat at the small table with me and grabbed a donut along with a section of the paper I'd been pretending to read. My mind had been focused on the words I was about to say, not the Times New Roman print on the page.

I studied Aila's face. She had no idea what she was about to hear.

Maybe she'd just think I was crazy.

Once she finished her donut and a glass of orange juice, I spoke.

"Aila. Before we get to Miami, or I guess before we leave today. There are some things you need to know about my brother and I. We're different."

"Of course you are—you're Romanian. There aren't many others from Romania in the U.S." Aila replied innocently.

I hated myself for what I was about to do. I had to do it. It was the right thing.

I took her hands in mine and looked her in the eyes.

"Aila, that ring you have . . . it's more powerful than you know. The monsters I told you about are real, but they aren't from the sea. They all used to be human . . . and they drink blood. Your ring protects you from vampires."

Aila remained silent as if she were trying to decide if I were insane or trying to be funny. She glanced at her ring with questioning eyes and back at me with the same expression.

"I don't get it," she said.

"As long as you wear that, no vampire can harm you. My brother can't harm you—I can't harm you. That's why you must never take it off."

"What are you saying? Is this some sort of joke? Maybe I'm just tired and that's why I'm not getting it," she said as her hands slipped out of my grasp. I feared it was the last time I would touch her. I had to be clear, even though it would hurt and confuse her.

"No, Aila. It's not a joke. I drink blood. I wanted to drink yours. Andrei will want to drink your blood if he ever meets you. I'm a vampire and I can prove it, but I don't want to scare you. That's why I'm telling you now. He'll try to tear us apart, but I know you are the one to break my curse."

"You aren't making any sense," Aila said.

"I know it doesn't make sense to you, but I can explain it all. I just need you to trust me first."

"I trust you," Aila said slowly. She seemed to regret the words as she said them but then processed another thought. "How would you prove it?"

"There are a few ways. The easiest would be if I showed you my fangs, but I don't know if it's a good idea. Don't worry—I have sworn to myself I would not drink from you. I don't want to drink human blood anymore, but it's the only way I can survive right now."

Aila seemed to think it over for a moment. She hadn't suspected anything. I sensed that her whole point of view on everything was changing. I remembered the way I reacted to the news that I was a vampire all those years ago. Now it was Aila's turn to react.

I didn't know if it would be in a good way or a disastrous way.

Her words came out calmly when she said, "I think I want you to show me. Not because I think you're crazy, but to prove to myself that I am not crazy for believing you."

"Are you sure?"

"Yes, I'm ready."

I opened my mouth and tried to bring out my fangs as slow as possible to show her I had control and to try to avoid scaring her. I watched her face as her curiosity peeked. She stared at my fangs for a long moment with her mouth wide open.

"I felt it," she said.

I retracted my fangs and asked, "Felt what?"

"I felt the ring push you away. First at the desk . . . and then again in the elevator . . . and when I went to your room to help you with the thermostat. I didn't wear it on our first date. Then I felt it when you picked me up for our second date. Last night. You had me take it off at the museum . . . oh, my."

"Yes, I did, but I returned it to you."

"Yes, but you had so many chances. Why didn't you . . ."

"I wanted to, but I just couldn't. You were too perfect. You are too perfect. I can't ruin the one thing that has brought me humanity in the last 250 years," I replied.

"250 years?"

Aila looked as though she would faint. "Why can't I feel the ring push you away now?"

"Because, my will not to harm you is strong enough that the ring can let down its barrier. If my brain were to switch back to the way it was before, the ring would instantly sense it and keep me away," I explained. "I can feel it now. It's because you have some fear of me now."

"And that little burst last night when you . . ." She trailed off, but I knew what she was talking about.

Aila looked at her ring and moved to take it off.

"No. Keep it on. I can't trust myself yet and I certainly can't trust any other vampires that may be lurking around."

"Others? Are there a lot of you?"

"There aren't billions of us or anything—more like a few hundred thousand, possibly a million, but you never know when you'll run into one, especially in a big city," I replied.

"Why are you telling me this?" Aila asked. She stood up and began to pace a little.

I sighed, what I was going to say might be even more difficult for me than telling her I was a vampire.

"I'm falling in love with you, Aila. My curse forces me to introduce you to my brother if we want to go any further. You don't have to meet him if you don't want to. He's much more deviant than I. He will do what he wants and he's ruthless. I'm telling you this in the hopes that you might run and never look back. This path is dangerous and I know I can't let him persuade you into a corner—or worse, make you join our ranks."

"What curse?"

"My brother and I have both been cursed by a witch. The only way to break the spell is for one of us to find a woman who loves him for everything he is. You see, from 1910 to 2010 we were in a deep slumber. We only have five years to find the one to break the curse or we will sleep for another 100 years. Even if you do feel the same way about me, my priority is to keep you safe. If that means I can never see you again, then so be it. If you were wise, you would leave me today and forget we ever met."

Aila crossed her arms and sat back at the table.

"I'll never forget meeting you, Dorin. I'm . . . I thought I was falling in love with you too."

The way she changed her words made my heart sink, but I continued.

"Aila, there's so much you don't know. There's so much I've done that would make you want to stay far away from me. I've killed, Aila. Innocent people have died in my hands, even women. No children, but plenty of women. I haven't killed a woman since waking up, but I've still taken their blood against their will and brought many to the brink of death."

"But you've changed?" Aila asked hopefully.

"Yes, but it doesn't erase what I've done. I was going to take your blood too. I could've killed you. Until a few days ago, no one was safe from me. The only reason I hadn't killed anyone since my awakening is because it's harder to cover your tracks these days. When I met you and spent time with you I began to feel things I hadn't felt since I was human. I have a new reason for not wanting to be a killer—a monster."

Aila seemed to think carefully about her next question. "Why did the witch curse you?"

"Andrei and I were in a sort of competition to get her to marry one of us. It was Andrei's idea, but that doesn't excuse my participation. The contest was to see which one of us could make a stranger fall in love with us first. The winner would have the freedom to ask the witch to marry him while the loser would step aside. When she found out what we were doing and furthermore, that the women we'd chosen were very dear to her, she was furious.

She didn't have the power to take away our ability to drink from women completely, but she could put restrictions on what we had to do in order to drink the blood of a woman. She deemed that any woman naïve enough to kiss one of us should fall prey to us. In an attempt to render our charm useless, she put us into a deep slumber for one hundred years in hopes that our charming ways would not affect the women of the future. She gave us until the next full moon to get ourselves in order.

Three days later I was fast asleep in a cave with Andrei next to me. The hundred years went by slowly. All the while I could still hear things going on in the outside world through the rock and rubble. It was all a blur when I woke up. Andrei and I studied for a whole year to prepare for the outside, only leaving the cave to feed—a task that had indeed become much more difficult."

Aila listened with intensity. I was relieved that she hadn't run away yet.

I continued, "After our year of study, Andrei decided he wanted to go back to the U.S. We had visited it once a few years before the witch cursed us. He'd always talked of returning, so he came over here and I was left with the vineyard we own. I left it in good hands during our slumber. My friend, Tavian watched over it. He too is a vampire. He's running it as I speak."

"So why did you decide to come to America?" Aila asked.

"The five years is closing in on us. I wanted to convince my brother to come back to Romania for the impending slumber. Although, he is adamant about staying here, I think it's best that we were in the same place. He wants me to sleep here, but I don't think it's a good idea. Other vampires might be able to find us easier here."

Aila seemed to be soaking everything up. She also looked overwhelmed.

59

I sighed. She needed some space. "Maybe I should give you a little time to absorb all this," I said to her.

The blank look on her face disappeared as she looked up at my eyes.

"Yes, I think I need a few minutes alone."

I nodded and replied, "I'll go for a walk. I'll put up the "Do Not Disturb" sign. Just take it down when and if you want me to come back. If you're still here we can talk some more. If not, I wish you a happy life, Aila."

Aila nodded as I stepped out. Our future rested in her hands.

Aila

My head swirled. My first instinct was to pack up my things and leave. It was just too much. The fact that Dorin was a vampire and the curse that plagued him left me feeling sick and terrified at the same time.

The first guy I met after a string of bad relationships turned out to be an ancient vampire who has killed before and who wanted to drink my blood. The whole first date was a lie. It had been a plot to get me close to him.

With those thoughts, I started to pack frantically.

I couldn't do this.

I couldn't be with a man like Dorin. He was a wolf in sheep's clothing. I didn't know if he would really leave me alone if I decided to leave without another word. I knew too much about him—he might revive his murderous ways.

But the man I had become familiar with wasn't like that.

I couldn't believe he was the same man he described to me just a little while ago.

Nevertheless, I continued to pack. I threw things into my suitcase—my frustrations were being taken out on my luggage.

Emotion flooded my body to the point that I fell to the ground and became buried by an overwhelming need to just crumple into a ball. I didn't understand why I felt so compassionate toward him.

The fact that I was even feeling conflicted about walking out of the hotel and never looking back startled me. There was no other choice. I couldn't possibly stay and pretend everything was alright. I couldn't overlook the fact that he had hurt so many people before.

Still, something inside me said I was making the wrong decision as I took the "Do Not Disturb" sign off the door and left the room.

CHAPTER ELEVEN

Dorin

I made my way back to the hotel room. I chose not to use my x-ray vision as I approached the door. The sign had been taken down. My heart ached as I slid the key into its slot and pressed the handle down. My gut instinct said she wasn't in there. I pushed the door open.

Empty.

Her things were all missing. No trace of her could be found. She was nothing if not thorough. I'd learned that on our date to the museum at the EcoLab exhibit. She'd meticulously picked through the silt and debris. She'd done the same thing to the hotel room. Picking out each belonging and packing it away.

I'd never forget the time I spent with her. I'd never forget I lost the one. It wasn't just that she was the one that would break the spell. It was the fact that I'd felt things I thought were long gone—along with my humanity. The drive to see Andrei would be even longer now that I had to go it alone.

I felt like breaking something.

My anger toward Andrei, toward the witch, and toward the entire vampire race mounted. I wanted to place the blame on everyone else but myself.

Unfortunately, the truth bored a hole into my mind. If I'd only been a better man I may have had a chance with Aila. If I hadn't killed people I might have had a chance. I was the only one at fault. I let out an exhausted sigh as I sat in a chair and stared out the window.

Aila

I raced to the front desk with my bags and asked the clerk to call me a cab. I waited impatiently as I looked around for any sign of Dorin. I didn't know if he'd be furious or if he'd come after me.

I had a feeling he already knew I left. My foot tapped nervously and finally the cab pulled up. I rushed to it—even though no one was chasing me.

That's when I realized no one was chasing me. He wasn't tracking me down to kill me or even to drink my blood.

He was letting me go.

Part of me felt relieved and another part of me burst with disappointment. A fleeting vision of Dorin stalking into the lobby and stealing me away back to our room struck me and took my breath away. I shook the vision out of my head and peered back at the elevators—just in case.

That was all it took. I'd looked back.

I wanted to see him coming out of the elevator. I wanted my vision to come true. My feelings for him wouldn't go away. Not even after he told me the truth. I always ran away from my feelings.

Not this time.

Before I even knew what I was doing, emotion overtook my actions and I was back in the elevator with my luggage abandoned in the lobby.

Before I knew it, I was standing at the door to our room. I slid my key into the reader and opened the door quietly. Dorin sat in a chair with his back to me. His head hung low and rested in his hands.

"Just one question: you said you haven't killed a woman since waking up. Is that a result of the curse or did you stop on your own?"

Dorin turned to face me. Intense emotions flickered across his face as he looked me in the eyes and answered, "I stopped on my own. During the one-hundred years I spent asleep, it was as if the people I'd killed haunted me. I thought mostly of their demise and how I'd caused it. I didn't grow much of a conscience, but it started to blossom. You restored it fully," he replied.

I stood silent and processed what he'd said. I wondered if it was fate that brought us together. There was no other explanation for the way I felt. I took a deep breath before speaking again.

"You aren't going to sleep for another hundred years. I won't live that long. It's now or never. Everything in your past is just that—in your past. If you leave it in the past, then I don't care what you've done, as long as it stays there. I know people change. I know there are things that everyone has done they aren't proud of. If you were able to stop yourself from being a monster, then I believe you deserve a second chance. In just these last few days I've been able to be myself around you and I think there's a reason for that."

"You left," Dorin said. "What changed your mind?"

"I thought I could leave and never look back, but I looked back. I was about to jump into a cab, but I checked the elevator and the lobby. I hoped to see you. That's when I realized there has to be some sort of meaning behind all this. Something stopped you from hurting me. Something powerful pushed us together."

Dorin stood and crossed the room slowly.

"You think there's a reason we met," he said as he tentatively took my hand in his own.

I nodded my head. "Maybe that's what the witch wanted. Maybe she needed you to understand that there was another way and that taking the difficult path would not be easy, but it would be rewarding. Anyone can take the easy way out and turn into a monster, but only a few can go into the deepest depths of inhumanity and come out a good man. Maybe she knew I would be the one to bring back the man you were before," I replied. "I believe you're right," he said.

I wrapped my arms around him and he did the same to me.

"Where's your luggage?" he asked.

"Uh. Down in the lobby," I replied. "I didn't want to waste any time."

Dorin pulled out of our hug. "It's okay. We'll get it on our way out. Ready to meet my brother?"

I nodded, although the impending meeting made me uneasy, Dorin could get me through it.

CHAPTER TWELVE

Dorin

We made our way out to the car. Aila apologized to the cab that was called for her and tipped the driver for his time.

I loaded her belongings and mine into Bill's trunk with his help and soon we were on the road.

Aila and I remained silent for the most part. We were lost in our own thoughts.

Aila's theory came to the center of my mind. I believed she was correct. The witch wanted to give me and my brother a second chance, but she only left room for one of us to receive the second chance. Andrei wasn't going to go down without a fight and Aila would be in the middle of it. I couldn't let her be a casualty of a war between brothers.

"Aila, I know you think we can do this, but I don't want you to get hurt. Andrei is dangerous. He's more dangerous than I ever was. He'll find a way to get what he wants. He's cunning and will stop at nothing."

"You've forgotten that I deal with people like that every day at work. They may not be killers, but they're usually willing to do anything to make money. My job is to make sure my company makes it through negotiations unscathed. I can do this, Dorin. I can see through people like they were made of glass."

"I don't want to put you at risk."

"You aren't putting me at risk. I'm putting myself at risk. We'll be careful. I'll meet him, we'll get all this out on the table and then we'll figure things out from there."

I thought it over a moment. "We'll be careful?"

"Extremely."

"And when it's all done we'll get out of there and we can be together?"

"Yes, we can be together," Aila reassured me.

Aila

I stared out the car window as the terrain changed. Dorin was on edge. His fist was clenched and he sat rigidly in his seat. I tried to relax him by talking idly about random things like we had before any of this came about. When that didn't work, I started asking him questions about being a vampire.

"How did you become a vampire?" I asked.

Dorin sighed. "The story isn't a pretty one, but you need to know everything before the curse can be broken. Andrei was turned first. He was turned by the Vampire Emperor of the time to battle in a war. Andrei quickly turned out to be one of his best soldiers. So, naturally when Emperor Bantshire heard Andrei had a brother, he turned me too. I was enlisted in his army after my first drink.

"The process is difficult to describe. The vampire who turns another has to inject venom through his fangs and into the blood stream. After the venom enters your body, you become extremely weak until you drink human blood. If you wait too long, your ability to move starts to dissipate as if you experience rigor mortis while still alive.

"The first drink of blood kick starts your system again. The venom gets what it needs to make you stronger, faster, and able to sense things that eluded you before."

"That helped you and your brother in the war?" I asked.

"The war I fought in was a war you wouldn't find in history books. It was between two groups of vampires. One group, led by the late Emperor William Bantshire who wanted the second group—the rebel vampires—to acknowledge him as their leader. I was commissioned to kill the rebel vampires, and I did so very well. Ever since then, everything between my brother and I has been a competition. I was promoted through the ranks, so he worked his way up as well. It came easy to me. I was trusted by the Emperor and so Andrei desired his trust as well.

"When the war was finally over, the Emperor gave us each a chance to join what he called the Project. I decided to take some time off and Andrei followed. We'd promised to return once the Project gained its bearings, but the Emperor was replaced by another. A man I'd fought next to in the war named Heath Weatherly. He's still in power today, and I'm not sure whether he knows we have awakened or not. It's likely he doesn't care. As long as we don't hamper his plans, he will not interfere with our lives."

"So, you were created to be a soldier? You had no choice."

"By the time I knew what had happened to me, it was too late. I had no choice but to do the Emperor's bidding. He was known as a volatile being—merciless to those who crossed him," Dorin explained.

I was deep in thought. There were two hours until we arrived in Miami and I had so many more questions. I didn't know how to ask some of them.

"You said you were made stronger, faster, and your senses heightened? How does that work?"

"I can move in the blink of an eye. I can push a train with 40 cars along its track. I can hear your heart beat from the next room, see a fly from a mile away, smell the tiniest drop of blood inside of a closed vial, and taste a grain of salt in a gallon of water. In exchange for all these, my sense of touch isn't as strong as a human's is. I can't feel extreme temperatures like you can. I don't feel pain as much, but I do feel your touch. It sends me back to the time I was human." "Is that all you can do?" I asked.

"Well, there's one more thing, but before I tell you, I just want to assure you that I've never used this ability inappropriately. I can use sound waves as a sort of x-ray vision, to see into other rooms. Sort of like bat sonar, I suppose."

"Really? You said you've never used it inappropriately? Have you used it to see into a room I was in?"

"Yes, but just to make sure you were safe. I might be a bit protective of you. Please, believe me when I say I haven't seen anything you would deem inappropriate, only you doing menial things like brushing your teeth and combing your hair—and only for a few seconds at a time. Any longer would make me thirsty."

"I believe you. I'm just not sure how I feel about that. It's strange to me. You can spy on me anytime you want," I said.

"I'm sorry if I've made you uncomfortable or if you feel debased on any level," Dorin replied with an ashamed tone.

"It's not that. It's just—I'm kind of embarrassed at what you might see or what you have seen. Maybe next time you could give me some warning or something. Let me know when you want to check in on me and make sure I'm okay?"

Dorin smiled kindly. "I can do that, my dear."

"It is kinda sweet that you're so protective," I said with my own smile spreading on my face.

"I think it's adorable that you could be embarrassed by anything you do. You're so beautiful and graceful that I can't help but watch you when we're together."

"I've had my clumsy, embarrassing moments—believe me."

"What's your most embarrassing moment?" Dorin asked.

"I don't think I want to tell you that."

"I have to tell you everything you want to know about me—can't you tell me that one thing?"

"Maybe some other time. I'm not sure I want to relive that at the moment."

Dorin smiled and kissed my forehead.

"Alright, but someday I'd love to hear it. I want to know everything about you, Aila."

I smiled as I looked out the window to the Fort Lauderdale area and sunk back into Dorin's arms. We'd be in Miami in a matter of two hours, and I was unsure how I felt about meeting Andrei. From Dorin's words, he'd be someone I didn't like and shouldn't trust. I thought of all the corporate executives I met before—most of which I couldn't trust. If I played it like a corporate negotiation, I'd be okay. All corporate meetings were dealt with by being polite yet firm. If there was anyone in the world who could go up against Dorin's brother and come away unscathed, it was me.

I started to think that maybe the witch had somehow known that I'd be born and knew Dorin would find me one day. Perhaps it was my destiny to help the witch give Dorin his second chance. She must have seen something in him, and cursed him to save him from his brother.

I didn't have much more time to think about it. We crossed into Miami city limits. Dorin seemed to go rigid again. He was afraid of how the meeting would go. It was nearing dinner time, so the plan was to have dinner at Andrei's house first and then check into the hotel.

"Are you sure you want to do this?"

"Yes, Dorin, I'm sure," I replied.

"Okay. Just make sure you don't trust him. Stay away from him if you can. I'll make sure you're sitting next to me at dinner. As far as his assistant goes, he's not bad, but you need to be careful around him too. Keep your ring on at all times and never let down your guard."

"Got it."

CHAPTER THIRTEEN

Dorin

"Let's venture into the lion's den," I said as I kissed Aila. Andrei's estate loomed in the car window.

Andrei's house was immense and situated on a large chunk of land overlooking the ocean. Andrei had been expecting us and was out on the driveway as soon as we pulled up. I took Aila's hand and helped her out of the car. We walked up to Andrei and his assistant.

"Andrei, this is Aila Myles, Aila this is my brother, Andrei."

"Pleased to meet you. Dorin has told me so much about you. I don't suppose he's talked much about me, but I'm sure you'll find out all you ever wanted to know about us in good time. I'm having dinner prepared for us. It should be ready soon. Would you like to take a short tour with my assistant while we wait? There's a matter I must discuss with Dorin."

"She can stay. Anything you have to tell me you can say in front of her, brother," I replied.

"I'll be fine, Dorin. I'd love to see the place, and you two haven't seen each other in such a long time. Don't worry about me," Aila said as Andrei's assistant came to stand beside her. I was uneasy about the situation, but Andrei's assistant wouldn't try anything, and she was wearing the ring.

Aila was swept away for her tour and I turned to Andrei with anger in my eyes. We both stood silent for a while.

"You better not be up to any of your tricks. I won't let you ruin this for me. If I have a chance at happiness I will take it. Why should we both be miserable for an eternity?" I asked.

"I want my chance too. It's my right. That's why the witch wanted to make sure we both meet her. I'll hand it to you— she's quite a treat. I could smell her the second the car door opened. Delicious," Andrei said.

"She's not food. She's mine."

Andrei chuckled. "You know, women of this century don't like it when you act like you own them. Perhaps I would be a better fit for her. We'll see who she picks."

"She must know the truth, so I told her. She knows the original competition was your idea. She knows you're the mastermind behind everything. She understands you and the last Emperor are the reason I'm a monster."

"The original competition?" Andrei repeated. We were locked in a staring contest. We heard Aila and the assistant approach from afar. "*O sa castig*," he added, meaning, I will win.

I glared at my brother. "*Nu e un concurs.*" It's not a competition.

"You possess a wonderful home," Aila said when she returned from her tour.

"Why thank you, Aila. How nice of you to say. Shall we go inside and see if dinner is ready?"

"Yes. Did you find a bottle of my wine, brother?" I asked as I placed my arm around Aila to show Andrei I wasn't going to back down.

73

"Actually, yes. I found several, and it's to be served with dinner."

"I can't wait," Aila replied.

Inside the large mansion was a wide open foyer. Just to the right was the dining room and lounge. The kitchen was closed off since Andrei had staff members to take care of the cooking and cleaning. Andrei lead the way to the table which was expertly set with a pale green runner and silver edged plates. If I could pay my brother one compliment, it would be that he knows how to hire good staff. There were glasses set out and a bottle of my wine ready to be poured.

The three of us sat. Andrei was at the head, I was on his right and Aila next to me. Andrei's assistant sat at his left—across from me. The wine was poured by a staff member and the appetizer plates were put down immediately after. I stopped Aila before she took a drink of her wine.

"Wait just a moment, my darling. I want to show you how to properly drink wine before you taste mine. I want to make sure you savor every part of it."

"Alright," Aila said with a smile.

"First, you observe the color. This red wine is my Feteasca Neagra. It is a very dark red, you'll notice. Now we swirl the wine in the glass and sniff the bouquet. Isn't it wonderful?"

Aila smelled her wine and agreed.

"There are so many layers to it."

"And now you may take a sip if you wish. Notice the blackcurrant flavor—like the sweetness of a berry. It's smooth and rich," I said.

Aila brought the glass to her lips and slowly tested the wine.

"Yes, you're right. It's excellent—the best wine I've ever tasted," Aila exclaimed.

Andrei sighed loudly and rolled his eyes. "Don't inflate his head even more than it already is. He does make good wine, but I do believe you are biased, my lady."

"I've tried every wine he's laid in front of me. All have been good, but his is the best," Aila replied.

Andrei merely smiled and nodded.

To complement the wine, we ate spaghetti and bread sticks, prepared by Andrei's private chef.

"Well, what shall we do tomorrow? I thought we could all head to Palm Beach for SunFest. Tomorrow is the opening ceremony," Andrei said.

"I don't think that's a good idea," I replied sharply.

"What's SunFest?" Aila asked.

"It's just a bunch of young people getting together to celebrate the beginning of summer. There are barbecues and concerts. It's really a fun time," Andrei replied.

Aila looked to me, likely wondering why I didn't like the idea.

I explained, "People like my brother and I think it's funny to go to SunFest because of the irony of it. Most humans think we can't go into the sun—those who believe anyway. It's become quite the tradition for vampires to show up at SunFest and they don't leave hungry."

"Oh, come on, she'll be with us. We're two ancient warrior vampires. Who's going to risk their eternal life for a snack?" Andrei asked.

I shook my head. "It's out of the question. Besides, Aila has to work tomorrow."

"What a pity," Andrei replied and promptly shoveled a bite of spaghetti into his mouth.

I caught the quick show of fangs Andrei displayed. Aila did too, and her heart rate quickened just a little. I glared at him in a warning fashion, but Andrei ignored me and grinned at Aila.

Aila

After dinner was over, Andrei told his assistant to show Dorin and me to our room.

"I think we'd planned to stay in a hotel," said Dorin.

"No, no, no," Andrei replied, "You should stay here. It's much more comfortable and it's free. Then we can all spend more time together."

"I don't think so. We wouldn't want to impose, brother," Dorin replied.

"Nonsense. There's no such thing when it comes to blood and those accompanied with blood, Dorin."

Andrei grinned at me. The expression reminded me of one I'd seen on Dorin's face during our first date. A sinister undertone to it pushed a sense of unease into my gut. Learning the truth about Dorin made me more aware of hints of deceit.

"The hotel is closer to Aila's meeting," Dorin replied.

"We do need to catch up. Not to mention Aila and I must get acquainted. What have you told her about the curse?" Andrei asked.

"I've told her everything," Dorin replied.

Andrei paused and looked me in the eyes before continuing. "The curse. It's a tricky one. That witch did a number on us, I'd say. Of course, the only part that really gets me is the part that says only one of us can be happy. One of us gets a second chance. Shall I recite the words?"

"I don't think that's necessary," Dorin replied.

"She must know all, brother," Andrei snapped. "I think that includes the words she spoke when she cast us into our doom. They are the words that will now ensure that my happiness is never found again. Aila, do you want to learn the curses she said to us?"

I didn't answer. Andrei stood and stared me in the eyes. His face resembled Dorin's, but even the familiarity couldn't mask the hate tugging at the corners of his eyes and pressing his lips together. He broke the expression as he spoke.

Before you drink the blood of a miss,
She must bestow on you a kiss.
It shall not be yours to take,
But her will to make.

Before you try your luck,
In your slumber you are stuck.
One hundred years you will sleep,
Half a decade to find one to keep.

This cycle shall repeat,
Until love the brothers meet.

One who knows the truth,

One who sees skin and tooth.

One loved, one forlorn,

One changed, one stubborn.

Keep your vengeance stubborn one,

Or stone you shall be in the sun.

Silence followed his emotional tirade. He spoke the words with anger, just as I assumed the witch spoke them. I could see Andrei's bitterness against the witch like a flag waving behind him. I could also understand he would not change his ways like Dorin had. He was never going to be the one that would break the spell.

It was always Dorin. I wondered if the witch had loved him in the way I was beginning to.

Andrei was the first to speak. "So, now you see that Dorin and I have been cursed by a cruel creature. Are you as cruel as she to leave me to my own misery and run off with my brother?"

Dorin stood from the couch with anger in his eyes.

"That is enough, Andrei." His voiced filled the large room and reverberated off the walls. I'd never heard him raise his voice in such a manner before.

He continued. "This is not her fault. We both knew you wouldn't change. You could have, but you lost your chance. If you're to be angry with someone you better be angry with me. She didn't know about the curse when she came into my life. How could she have chosen you when she didn't know you?

It seems unfair, but that's how it's going to be. I think Aila and I better leave."

Dorin took my hand and pulled me to a stand. We started walking away, but Andrei stopped us.

"The curse isn't broken yet. There are things she still doesn't know. Information even you aren't privy to. I'm the keeper of many secrets."

"I don't care. We're leaving. I can't have you scaring her—or worse, so we're leaving."

"Wait, Dorin," I said, "I have to know everything if we want to break the curse. If he has secrets, then we must get him to tell us."

Dorin's gaze snapped to Andrei and then back into my eyes. "It's not worth it. He'll hold them over our heads until it's too late," he replied.

My free hand found Dorin's other hand. I pulled both of our interlocking hands together between us and whispered, despite Andrei's superior hearing, "We have to try. I want to be with you. Two years isn't long enough. Let's try to negotiate or something."

"I don't like this," Dorin replied.

"I know. The second you think it won't work we can leave. We can figure something else out. If I have to be like you and wait a hundred years to see you again, I will," I replied.

Dorin's shock was plain on his face. "You will not have to do that. I don't want you to have to live like a monster. We'll stay on two conditions. One, we leave if I feel it's not going to work, and two, you promise me you won't ever try to become a vampire—even if we only have two years together."

I reluctantly agreed to the terms and we turned around to face Andrei. Dorin's rigid posture said he was extremely unhappy with the situation.

"She's going to have a dagger on her at all times along with her ring. So you better behave yourself," Dorin said to Andrei.

"Can't you see the halo and wings?" he replied, and then added, "One room, or two?"

"One," Dorin replied, "I'm not letting her out of my sight."

"Very well, Victor? Show them to the guest room. Shall we meet for discussing terms in about thirty minutes on the terrace?" he asked us. Dorin nodded and we watched as Andrei retreated to his study.

Victor led us to the guest room which was rather large and luxurious. There was one king sized bed draped in deep red, silky furnishings, from the large mattress to the canopy over the bed. There was a flat screen hi-def television and a large couch that matched the color of the bed linens. The tables all looked genuinely antique with dark wood that matched the wood floors.

There was an attached bathroom which was also very large and filled with fine linens and fluffy white towels. The bathroom looked like a personal spa. A massive claw-foot bathtub was at the center. I loved claw-foot bathtubs. I tried to conceal my enjoyment of the amenities since I knew Dorin was unhappy that we had to stay.

I watched as Dorin rummaged through his bag and came up with a black, pointy object. He walked toward me and slipped it into my hands. I looked curiously at him before asking, "What is this?"

"It's a dagger made out of obsidian. Obsidian is the only thing that can kill a vampire. If Andrei tries anything, I want you to stab him in the chest with it. It must pierce his heart to kill him. Anything else will just injure him and we heal very quickly."

I looked down at the sharp object. It was black and smooth with edges that reminded me of a Native American arrowhead. I ran my finger along the edge to test the sharpness. I'd never stabbed anyone before and I wasn't sure if I could.

"Promise me you'll fight if he tries anything," Dorin said.

"I don't know if I can stab another person. Self-defense is a common thing that must be done at times, but I don't think I could react quickly enough. Of course, I'll try, but from what you've said, I won't even have time to flinch."

"That's why you have the ring. The dagger is a secondary precaution. The ring should protect you, but there are indirect ways Andrei could get around the ring. That's when you use this," Dorin replied.

"Okay. I think I can do that," I said. I was starting to feel the stress of being in the presence of a vampire that most likely wanted to drink my blood. I wanted to be strong for Dorin, so I put on a brave face as we headed out to the terrace to meet Andrei.

CHAPTER FOURTEEN

Dorin

Andrei was already on the terrace, lounging on one of the chairs and looking out at the grounds surrounding his home. The sugarcane crops were near Palm Beach and were left in the care of a manager. The breeze carried the refreshing scent of the ocean through the air. It was beginning to get dark and stars started to shimmer in the sky.

"Come. Sit," Andrei said as he gestured to the other chairs. Aila and I did so and faced him with stern looks on our faces. We knew he wanted something in return for helping us break the curse, but we had no idea what it could be.

"What is it you want?" I asked.

Andrei smiled and leaned forward with his elbows on his knees and his hands clasped together in front of him.

"There are a few things. First and foremost—I want a taste."

I heard Aila's heart skip a beat.

"Out of the question. Next?" I said quickly. I took her hand in mine and squeezed it.

"That's a deal breaker," Andrei replied as he leaned back in his seat and crossed his arms. "If I'm going to be miserable and unsatisfied for the rest of my eternal life, then I want a taste of her blood."

"It's not going to happen. I'll find you a thousand other women before I allow that."

Andrei looked to Aila. I saw her concern as well.

"I don't think she likes that idea. She's a rather compassionate one, isn't she?" Andrei asked.

"Don't worry, Aila. He doesn't need me to bring him a thousand women, he gets them himself. Isn't that right?"

"Alright, I'll put that one on the back burner—for now. I also want you to come with me to meet the Emperor tomorrow, while Aila's working," Andrei said.

"He'll be in town?" I asked incredulously.

"He'll be in Palm Beach. He wants to meet with us to discuss possible positions in his ranks. He wants both of us and I told him I'd try to bring you. If you don't come, he won't see me, and I do want a royal position on the Council if I'm not going to be sleeping for another hundred years."

"So that's the real reason you wanted to go to SunFest," I inserted.

"You got me. Can we move on? What's your answer?"

"What will you give in return?" I asked.

"I will give you one secret," Andrei replied.

"How many secrets do you have, brother?"

Andrei turned his gaze to Aila. "It won't matter if I don't get a taste from her."

My anger bubbled to the surface again. My muscles tensed and my fangs descended.

"What else do you want?" I said through clenched teeth.

"Hmm, you know, I think I'd like access to the archives in Romania. The ones under that house you have on the vineyard. The ones you said were given to you and you alone," Andrei replied.

"Done, I can have Tavian send over the books in the morning. I'll even overnight them if you want," I replied. I had no idea what he wanted with dusty old books written in witch symbols.

"Make the call and I'll reveal a secret right now, just to show you I'm serious about this whole thing," Andrei replied.

I nodded and made the call.

Tavian said it would take two days for them to be delivered since it was so late, which was good enough for Andrei. He smiled as he decided which secret to tell.

"Ah yes, do you remember the witch that cursed us? Tallia?"

"Of course I do," I said, annoyed at his ridiculous question.

"Well, another reason she was so angry with me, was because I drank from her. I'd persuaded her to let me drink from her in return for putting in a good word for her with the Emperor. I never put in the good word, so she was quite angry with me and she took it out on you too," Andrei replied.

"Why the hell would you do that?" I yelled.

"Because I wanted to see what witch blood tasted like. It's very good by the way. A delicacy, and it makes you feel so powerful," he added. "I bet Aila's blood would taste just as good—if not better."

I clenched my fist. I didn't need another reason to want to punch him. He was pushing his luck. I held back for Aila's sake and settled for a verbal warning.

"Andrei, it's not going to happen, so stop bringing it up!"

Aila

My thoughts were going a mile a minute. Andrei wasn't going to let this issue drop, but the thought of him drinking my blood made me want to pass out. I'd given blood before at a few blood drives at work, but that was with a needle and a vial . . . and a professional phlebotomist. That's when I hatched an idea.

"How do you want the blood? Does it have to be directly from me or can it be in a vial?"

"Aila, no," Dorin said with wide eyes.

"I want the experience. I want it directly from you. It doesn't taste as good from a vial. It would be like drinking wine out of a paper cup," Andrei explained.

Dorin was clearly furious now. Drinking from me would mean I'd have to kiss him, and that was probably as much of a trigger as the blood drinking.

"Stop. We are not discussing this anymore. There will be no drinking from Aila. That is final. Are you going to substitute that for something else or are we wasting our time?"

"I don't know. I'm desperate to have it. Give me some time to come up with something equally tantalizing. I'll let you know tomorrow morning before Aila goes to work. Is that fair enough?"

"I suppose. I don't want any of your games, Andrei. You tell me what you want tomorrow morning or I'll make sure you never see the archives. I still have time to intercept the package and burn everything in them," Dorin warned.

"Understood. Now, I'm afraid it's time for me to enjoy a real meal. Excuse me, and enjoy your suite," Andrei said.

Dorin took my hand and led me to our room without another word uttered from either of the vampires.

Once inside our room, I noticed Dorin's agitated state. I didn't know what to do to calm him down. I watched as he paced the room back and forth. I wondered if I'd done or said something wrong.

I retreated to the bathroom to let him cool off. I couldn't help but let a tear slip from my eye. I was stressed. This was a negotiation I wasn't sure I could handle after all. There was so much I didn't know and so little I could do to help. I'd left the door open and before the stray tear could tumble down my cheek and leap from my chin, Dorin was there to catch it.

"I'm sorry, my love. I shouldn't have put you through this," Dorin said as he embraced me. I enjoyed the warm hug. He wasn't mad at me—he was as frustrated by the situation as I was. Our life together was in the hands of his wicked brother and whether or not we'd make it out on top was questionable.

"It's not your fault, Dorin. I want to be here. I want to fight. Remember? I told you I wanted to fight. This is what I'm supposed to do. I can feel it," I replied.

We embraced for a while longer and Dorin swept me up and carried me to the bed. We kissed until I lost my breath. I wanted more, but I couldn't allow myself to go too far quite yet. I had to tread carefully. I'd been hurt before and although Dorin was no ordinary man, I still had to guard myself.

Dorin seemed to pick up on my reluctance and stayed away from areas that would put us both into a frenzy. He playfully nibbled at my ear and kissed my neck. His lips on my neck and the fact that he was a vampire sent a brief wave of panic through me and the ring put out a short burst of energy that we both felt. I smiled and Dorin chuckled a little before continuing with his gentle exploration of me. He ran his fingers along my collarbone and then swept his fingers under my shirt to expose my shoulder.

I ran my hand along the back of his neck and into his hair. I tangled the dark tendrils in my fingers. His eyes grew dark and he held me tighter. I kissed him more and more, until the urge to go further threatened to take control of my body.

I lightly applied the brakes, or, at least, took my foot off of the accelerator by removing my fingers from his smooth hair and running them down his back.

"Aila," he moaned.

"Yes?" I whispered as he stopped kissing me and looked me in the eyes.

"I want you. I want you, but I know the timing is too soon. I promise to be patient if you promise not to make my blood sizzle like this until we're ready. It's hard to stop the feral instincts. I don't want them to take over."

"Okay, but can we still kiss?"

"Yes, just no hair pulling and you are restricted to kissing my lips only."

"That's not fair, you get to kiss my neck," I lightly complained.

Dorin smiled, "I better not do that anymore. At least for the time being. Besides, you better get some sleep. It's getting late."

I nodded and looked toward the nightstand. There was no alarm clock. I looked toward the other and saw the same thing—no alarm clock.

"Uh, there's no alarm," I stated.

"Oh. I guess that's what you get when you stay in a house where no one sleeps. Don't worry. I'll wake you up."

I smiled and nodded while I let out a yawn. I went to the bathroom to put on my pajamas and brush my teeth. I returned and pulled the covers back.

"Is cuddling off-limits?" I asked. Dorin grinned and joined me on the bed, "Definitely not."

After a good sleep, I woke to Dorin's perfect face. I smiled at his gentle waking and then my nostrils caught scent of something marvelous—French toast.

"Good morning," I said with a smile.

"I've become a horrible cook, so I had the chef make this for you," Dorin replied.

I munched down my breakfast and then went through my morning routine to get ready. It was my last day of work before my vacation. I hoped I could focus on the meetings I had set for the day and not on the mess Dorin and I were in. I wondered if Dorin was still planning to go see the Emperor even if Andrei decided there was no substitute for my blood. My unasked question was quickly answered.

"I want you to be extremely careful. As it turns out, Tavian decided to hop on a plane, so I'm leaving him here in Miami with you while I go see what the Emperor wants. He'll keep his distance and watch for any other vampires in the area. Although, I'm sure they're all in Palm Beach. If you need help, he will be there in a flash. You probably won't even notice him. He should be here just about the time you have to leave for your meetings. I'll drop you off and he'll take it from there."

"And Andrei?"

"He's decided he can deal with not drinking from you, although he's not sure what he wants yet. I'm sure I'll find out soon. You have your dagger, right?"

"Yes, I'm going to keep it in my purse. The cool thing about an obsidian dagger is it won't set off a metal detector," I added with a small smile.

"If I'm not back by the time you get off of work, Tavian will bring you here. Just wait here until I return, alright?"

I nodded and prepared myself for the long day ahead without the company of Dorin.

CHAPTER FIFTEEN

Dorin

I waved goodbye to Aila after I introduced her to Tavian and felt comfortable he would protect her. Tavian had developed a taste for animal blood while I was in my slumber, so he was off human blood for good. It had been almost seventy years since Tavian drank from a human or even tasted human blood.

I instructed my driver to go back to the house to pick up Andrei. I hadn't wanted my brother to be aware of Tavian's presence, so Andrei stayed home while I saw Aila off to work. Within thirty minutes or so, we pulled back into the long drive of Andrei's estate. He'd been waiting and immediately got into the car.

"What took so long?" he complained. "The Emperor expects us in less than two hours. I hope the morning traffic has died down by now."

It would be a long drive to Palm Beach.

"Oh, and I put in an application for two drudges. I listed you as a reference and although I doubt he'll ask you—one of my conditions for information is that you give me a good reference if he does ask you about it."

"Very well," I replied. I didn't know why Andrei wanted two drudges, but it was no concern of mine for the time being.

I just wanted to break the curse and begin my new life with Aila.

Nearly two hours of Andrei's babbling later, we arrived in Palm Beach and quickly navigated our way to the place the Emperor was staying. He kept a large estate in West Palm Beach. It seemed to be a larger version of Andrei's estate and worth twice as much.

We pulled into the drive. Two guardians and two drudges came out to greet us with a good frisk to make sure Andrei and I weren't carrying anything that could harm the Emperor. We were then lead into the large mansion and to the back of the building where the Emperor and his Empress lounged by the pool.

"Ah! My friends!" the Emperor exclaimed. He stood and shook our hands. "So glad you could make it!"

"We're glad to be here," Andrei spoke.

"Yes, and intrigued," I added.

"I'm sure you're wondering why I asked you here. You see, very soon, two spots on the advisory council will be . . . opening up, and I heard that you fellows might be close to breaking the curse set upon you by the witch, Tallia."

I tried to conceal my mortification over the Emperor knowing about Aila and I. Andrei must have told him. Of course, that's why we were here. The Emperor had never bothered to ask us to be on the council before since it would have been a waste of time.

"I understand you found a woman that suits you? A human woman?" he asked me. I simply nodded.

"No need to be shy about it. We all know the story of my weakness for a certain human girl who stole my heart," Heath said as he turned to his wife and Empress, Iris. "It happens. I assume you plan to turn her?"

I didn't want to tell him I had no such plans, so I fibbed a little. "We haven't gotten that far yet. I want to make sure we can break the curse before I do anything of the sort. There are plenty of hoops to jump through before the curse is fully broken."

"I sense your reluctance. I want you to know I've been there. I didn't want to turn Iris, but ultimately it was the only way we could be together. Isn't that right, Iris?"

"If he wouldn't have turned me, I would have found a way to become a vampire myself. That's how much I love him. I couldn't stand the thought of us being apart. I'm willing to bet your Aila would do the same. I'd love to meet her. She sounds so much like me. I could give her some pointers since I've been in her shoes before."

I smiled. "I'm sure she would like that."

I didn't like that they already knew her name. If they knew that, they could know so much more, which made me very uncomfortable.

Heath walked toward the pool and turned around to face me and Andrei again. "I'm running out of people I can trust. The two of you fought next to me during the war. I trusted you both with my eternal life and I want both of you on the council once I take care of my business and you take care of yours. The deal is that it has to be both of you. I feel that you balance each other out well. You complement the thoughts and actions of the other. We are about to do something big. Granted it will take roughly seven years until the Project will be in full swing, but I want you both to be part of it."

"The Project? You mean Bantshire's project is still going?" I asked.

"Yes, I found his plans. Very interesting. A few years ago, the opportunity to turn The Project into reality fell into my lap. I plan to carry on the only good idea he ever had."

"It's definitely something to consider," I replied. I always wondered what the Project was. Rumors said it would make life as a vampire much easier.

"Of course, don't give me an answer now. Wait until the curse is fully broken. By then I should have my problems dealt with. As for the rest of the day, since you came all this way, I'd like to give you a tour of the new Psytech branch I've opened here in Palm Beach. That will give you a feel for what I'm talking about."

"That would be excellent!" Andrei replied eagerly. I was less than enthusiastic about spending the day with the Emperor. Not that I didn't like him—I just wanted to get back to Miami. I knew Tavian would be watching out for Aila, but not being able to do it myself was eating away at me. Tavian would be at the estate until he saw me return, but somehow it didn't seem like enough.

The tour of the new Psytech facility was long and tedious. I didn't care much for technology or the Emperor's plans for the vampire race to profit from it.

Andrei, on the other hand, was enthralled by everything the Emperor said. I only listened to make sure I didn't miss anything important. If Andrei got his way I'd have to serve on the council, which would be a position I'd need to take seriously in order to stay favored by Heath. He had the power to demand Aila to be turned into a vampire, but he also had the power to look the other way.

Luckily, the council wasn't hard work. It converged for one month of each year to tour facilities and track the Psytech projects the Emperor supervised. Most facilities ran smoothly, developing gadgets and new high-tech software. Each facility had a full-time president to oversee most operations. At the end of the month of meetings, the council would advise the Emperor on what to do next. The Emperor would call random meetings throughout each year which would only last a day or so.

My indifference no doubt annoyed Andrei, but I didn't care about Andrei's feelings. I just wanted to get back to Miami to see Aila, but the Emperor would keep us as long as he wanted. If I tried to leave his presence prematurely, the Emperor would no doubt see it as reluctance to be part of the royal society and therefore, I would become a target for exile and Aila would become a target for hungry vampires. If I was exiled, my relationship with Aila would not be sanctioned by the Emperor and she would be hunted down. The only reason she was allowed to know about the vampire world and still be human was because of mine and Heath's past. If he wanted to, he could make me turn her with just a few words from his mouth.

"Well, it seems we have one more business matter to discuss before we can enjoy ourselves at the opening ceremony of SunFest. Andrei, I received your application for the approval of two drudges put into your care and training, and I see you listed Dorin as your reference. Of course, I know that you're a good fit for the further training of our drudges and if these two go well I'd like to put more in your care. I just need a signature from Dorin saying that he approves of my decision and we can get you two drudges fresh out of boot camp. Dorin?"

The Emperor motioned for one of his assistants to bring forward the approval form. I was handed a pen and I saw no reason to deny my brother two drudges. If they became a problem I would simply dispose of the pathetic humans and answer to the Emperor later.

"Thank you, Emperor. Thank you, Dorin. I shall do my best to train them right," Andrei replied.

"Call me Heath, Andrei. We fought side by side for years. We're the same age. There's no reason for the formalities.

Besides, we all know the real reason I took this job—to get rid of that wretched Bantshire!" he laughed and Andrei and I chuckled as well. Heath's overthrow had gone down in history as one of the most well-thought-out vampire dethronements there ever was.

I looked to Iris who was enjoying a manicure by the pool. She'd been the key to Heath's plan. She was quite the actress, which made me wonder if she'd been acting when she said she wanted to meet Aila. There'd be no reason for her to hurt Aila, but something didn't seem right about Iris. She'd become much too accustomed to the royal life—to the life of the vampire. She acted as if all should worship her.

"Alright, now that all the business is behind us, shall we go enjoy a late lunch and then head over to opening ceremonies?" Heath asked.

"That sounds good to me. Dorin? Shall we?" Andrei turned to him.

"Of course, a good steak sounds appetizing," I replied.

Aila

My meetings dragged on. I kept glancing at the clock or my phone. Time seemed to stand still. I wondered if I was being crazy. I barely left Dorin's side since we met, but surely I could handle a few hours away from him.

I did worry about his meeting with the Emperor. The way Dorin spoke of him made me uneasy. It was as if he had too much power over him. I didn't like that.

Tavian seemed to lurk just out of sight everywhere I went. The meetings had me running all over the corporate area of the city. Hotel conference rooms, restaurants, and office buildings were the venues for important negotiations for my company.

All I wanted to do was see Dorin. I couldn't wait to be in his presence again.

CHAPTER SIXTEEN

Dorin

The three of us ate lunch at a local restaurant and then headed to the beach for the 4 o'clock opening ceremony of SunFest. The place was crawling with vampires. I noticed them all in the form of pale skin and some with the tell-tale bright green eyes of a new vampire. They were in the crowds and on the buildings. A few familiar faces stood out, but none to make me want to chat. The ceremony dragged on. People were screaming and getting drunk. A few intoxicated men walked past Andrei, Heath and I. One was shoved into Heath by another. My nerves tingled. I wasn't sure how Heath would react.

"I suggest you boys get going. Perhaps you should slow down the drinking a bit," Heath said in a low voice.

"I suggest you get going," one of them said.

"I don't think you want to pick a fight with me and my friends here. Move along," the Emperor countered.

The last thing I wanted was to have to take care of three dead bodies and delay my return to Miami even more. I groaned inside. Andrei seemed eager to take them on alongside Heath.

"You can't tell me what to do! I'll punch your face in!" the same one replied. The other two laughed and sized up Andrei and me.

The problem was, no matter what they decided, they didn't know what our trio of vampires were capable of. We'd all fought in the vampire war and we all survived. That was enough to make other vampires afraid of us. Tearing apart three drunken men would be like tearing into the tender steaks we had for lunch.

Heath smiled. "I'd like to see you try."

The one confronting Heath wound up and punched the Emperor square in the jaw. He didn't even flinch. His face was in the same position showcasing the same evil grin when the human pulled his hand away. The human's face scrunched in pain. The heart rate of the three humans jumped. The fumble left them frazzled.

"My turn," Heath said before he punched the human square in the chest. He didn't use as much force as he could have since a crowd was starting to form, but he knocked the human flat on his back and no-doubt removed the air from his lungs. He coughed and gasped for breath. The man was lucky to be alive. Heath caught sight of a patrolman and watched as the other two men grabbed the winded man in the sand and dragged him off.

"Perhaps we should go," Heath said.

"I agree," I replied with relief. Andrei seemed a little disappointed. It was beginning to get late. The sun began its descent in the sky, and we still had a two-hour drive back to Miami. I discreetly sent Aila a text message saying I was trying to get back soon and that I'd have to stop at the blood bank before seeing her. I hadn't drunk any blood the night before and I could feel my thirst creeping up on me.

We all piled into Heath's limo. He instructed the driver to go back to the estate so Andrei and I could be on our way.

"Don't make it another hundred years before I see you two again," Heath joked.

"We're trying our best not to," I replied with a smile.

Moments later, we arrived at the estate and we said our good-byes before hopping into my hired car again. It was almost 6 o'clock. I told Andrei to call his chef and have him cook a meal for Aila. He reluctantly obliged and made the call.

"Alright. You know what I want. I want to be on the council. That means you have to be on the council too. That's what I will substitute for the delectable blood of your dear Aila. Deal?" Andrei asked with his hand outstretched.

I agreed and shook Andrei's hand. "You have a deal. No more talk about Aila's blood and I will join the council once the curse is broken. That means you must reveal a secret, so let's talk about that."

"Alright, that seems fair enough. I'll tell you this one since it directly affects you and then you can relay it to her. Remember how I told you the old Emperor already knew I had a brother? That if I didn't give up your whereabouts, he'd kill our mother?"

I didn't know where this was going, but it couldn't be anywhere good.

"Yes," I replied.

"Well, he didn't know about you until I told him. He offered me a promotion if I could find someone with my skills. I gave you up. Isn't that funny?"

I always had a feeling the truth wasn't so far from what Andrei just told me, but hearing it after all these years made my blood boil. I balled up my fist and punched Andrei. His head hit the passenger window and cracked it.

Andrei smiled as the small wound healed itself. "I figured you'd react that way. Feel better now?"

"Sorry, Bill. I'll replace that," I said to the driver.

"No problem, sir," he replied. I detected a faint smirk. He knew Andrei deserved it.

Bill was a new vampire who'd just finished his two-year study and was working his way up. Driving around older vampires was a way of getting connected, and after all he'd done for me I was going to put in a good word for him. Andrei's smirk didn't wear off for the rest of the trip. I didn't say a word to him. I was too angry to even look at him and spent most of the drive looking out my own window.

Once we entered Miami limits, I had Bill drop me at the nearest blood bank. I told him to take Andrei wherever he wanted to go and then come back for me. Then I messaged Tavian to tell him to stay put for now and patrol the house to make sure Andrei behaved and to call me if he tried anything.

Aila

"Aila, there you are, I've been looking for you," Andrei said from behind me. I was admiring some of the art in the living area of Andrei's house after a long day of meetings.

"Andrei, you scared me. Where's Dorin? I thought the two of you were returning from Palm Beach together."

Andrei stepped closer. "We did. He got hung up on the way back, something about needing a kosher drink."

"Oh, right. I almost forgot. Well, I guess I better wait for him in our room. I'm getting tired anyway," I said.

"Dorin and I spoke. I'm being supportive now. It's been a long time since either of us has been happy and I'm glad one of us can find some joy in this world. I told Dorin I was being selfish when I said all those things. Please, join me for a little peace offering—a glass of Dorin's wine?"

"I suppose one glass would be alright. I'm really sorry about this whole thing. I do feel bad that you'll be miserable, but maybe that part of the curse won't be true. Maybe if you change too you can also be happy," I said as Andrei poured a glass of wine for me.

"Perhaps, but I do like the way I live my life now. I hope it doesn't change too much. At least I won't have to sleep for another hundred years before I wake again. I'll tell you, I don't want to study for a whole year straight again before coming out. That's the part I despised the most."

"Dorin told me about that," I said as I took a sip of my wine.

"Yes, well, we didn't want to appear as complete idiots. If we still talked and behaved like we were from the last century, people might wonder."

"Of course. You know, you two are very much alike in some ways and completely opposite in others. It's interesting."

"Our mother always said he inherited his personality from her and I from our father. She said the elements that made up her and my father's love were the only similarities my brother and I shared. My father agreed."

"I have gotten the sense that Dorin is rather fond of your mother. I wish I could have met her," I said.

"You're like her in many ways. It' probably why Dorin is so drawn to you," Andrei replied.

I smiled at the compliment and took another sip.

"It's strange. Before I met you—before I knew about any of this—I had a dream about you and Dorin in a restaurant with me. The two of you started to fight and there was nothing I could do. That's all I remember, though. I never got to see if you made up."

"Well, I believe you can see that now. We've been on good terms today."

I smiled, but I was starting to feel tipsy already. "Would you excuse me a moment? I ate dinner, but I think I need to eat something else. This wine is really hitting me hard."

Andrei smiled and said, "Of course, there are some breadsticks on the counter, I think I'd like some too if you would be so kind as to bring them back. Help yourself to anything else you want, my dear. You're welcome to anything at all."

I nodded and headed to the kitchen. The room spun and I had to hold on to the counter to keep from falling. I'd never gotten drunk off of such a small amount before. The kitchen door opened and Dorin stepped in. His figure blurred, but I could sense it was him before he spoke.

"Aila! Where's Andrei?"

I could only point.

"What's wrong?"

"I don't know . . . I feel . . . dizzy," I said before falling into his arms.

CHAPTER SEVENTEEN

Dorin

I looked into Aila's eyes with her limp body draped over my arms. Her pupils were dilated. "He's drugged you! I'll kill him!"

"Peace offering," she mumbled.

I carried Aila to the nearest chair and sat her in my lap, holding her by the shoulders.

"Aila, try to stay awake, darling. Stay awake," I said to her, although it didn't do much good. She was getting closer and closer to losing consciousness. Andrei walked in the room and sighed.

"Must you ruin everything?" he asked.

"What were you thinking? If she dies—you die. I don't care if I need you alive to break the curse—you will die. What did you give her?"

"Oh calm down, she's not going to die. It was just a little GHB. You're being overly dramatic. It's nothing I haven't used before. Although I think I should have dropped the dose. I forgot she's not as tolerant to narcotics as the women I'm used to."

"We're leaving. I'm done with you, Andrei. This isn't a game!"

"Oh, come on. I just wanted a taste—I wasn't going to kill her."

"No. You went too far this time. I'm finished with you. I don't care if I ever see you again. If I do, I might just kill you anyway for even thinking about drinking from her. You can say goodbye to the position on the council. If the curse is broken I won't serve with you."

I picked Aila up and stormed out of the kitchen door to the car. Bill had been waiting for my instructions. I gently sat Aila in the car and climbed in after her.

"Bill, can you find us a decent hotel?"

"Sure thing, sir."

I turned my attention back to Aila who was still barely conscious. I knew from my year of study that GHB was dangerous and I needed to listen for signs of respiratory distress.

So far, Aila's breathing remained normal, but her lifeless body could barely sit up in the seat.

"I don't know what would have happened if I wouldn't have come back in time. Aila, I'm so sorry," I whispered. Although, she probably wouldn't remember much from the night. I should have let Tavian interfere when Andrei decided to come back to the house instead of going out to the clubs he frequented.

Aila mumbled something I couldn't make out and tried to lay down in my lap. "No, Aila, I need you to stay awake until I can be sure that you'll be okay."

"Sleepy," she mumbled.

"I know, my darling, just a little while longer and you can go to sleep."

Most of the decent hotels in Miami were full. Bill called a few in West Palm Beach and finally found one with an opening.

It only took Bill an hour to drive what would normally take almost two. Aila had been somewhat lucid during the car ride, but she uttered words that made no sense and acted lethargically. We pulled up to the hotel and I asked Bill to go inside and get two rooms. Moments later, he returned and handed me a set of keys and my wallet.

"They asked that you come down and sign something before too long," he reported.

"Of course, thank you. Would you pull around to the side entrance?" I asked. Bill nodded and put the car into drive. I carried Aila up to the second floor where we had a suite with two beds. Bill went to his own room across the hall.

I laid her on the bed and listened to her breathing for a moment to make sure it was still regular.

Her breathing turned out to be fine and she had her sleepy eyes open. Her gaze steadied on me for a moment and she smiled. "Dorin."

"Yes, it's Dorin. We're in a hotel. We won't be seeing Andrei again," I replied.

"Kiss me," she half mumbled.

I leaned down and kissed her forehead. Before I could pull away she began to pull my lips to hers. I allowed one kiss before I tried to disentangle myself.

"Darling, you need to rest."

"No, I feel so awake now. I want to do something. I want to kiss you all over!"

"Aila, it's not right. You've been drugged and I won't take advantage of you. Nothing of that sort will happen until every ounce of that stuff is out of your system."

"But, I want to. You're so sexy. I've thought that ever since I first saw you. Come on, come lay with me," Aila said, patting the bed next to her. I grinned, now that she was saying full sentences she'd be okay, but for the time being she'd be a little loopy.

"Very tempting, but I think I'll stay over here. In fact, I have to go down to the front desk to sign something. I wager you'll be asleep by the time I return."

She smiled and sat Indian-style on the bed.

"Okay, let's make a deal. If I'm awake, we do what I want to do when you get back. If I'm asleep, then you win and tomorrow I'll tell you the answer to that question you asked—about my most embarrassing moment."

I smiled. "Deal. I'll be right back."

"Okay! I'll be waiting! Wide awake!" she said with a little wave of her hand.

I closed the door behind me and knocked on Bill's door across the hall. I asked him to keep an ear out for anything unusual. He obliged, so I headed to the front desk.

I signed the sheet and thanked the clerk for allowing my driver to check in for me. She smiled and said it was no problem. I decided to play it safe and explore the hotel while I waited for Aila to fall asleep. I kept my ear tuned to that area of the hotel, but Bill was alert and Tavian lurked somewhere near for extra protection. After I saw the pool, the lounge, and the business and spa facilities, I made my way back to the room. I listened from outside the door to make sure she was asleep.

I opened the door to a sight that made me smile and fall even more in love with Aila. She was fast asleep with all her clothes on in the same spot I'd left her. Her breathing remained normal and I knew she'd be okay, but that didn't change how I felt about Andrei's betrayal. Something had to be done about him.

Aila

I woke with a pounding headache. Dorin sat quietly on the bed across from mine. When I moved, he instantly reacted.

"Aila, how are you feeling?"

I tested myself. I couldn't remember anything after my conversation with Andrei. The only ailment I had was the headache.

"Fine, I think. I just have a headache. What happened?"

"Andrei drugged you with GHB. He wanted to get you high so you'd take off your ring and kiss him so he could drink from you. Luckily, I got there before anything could happen. Tavian called me and said something was up. I instructed him to stay on the sidelines unless he tried anything and I came back to find you stumbling through the kitchen. We left Andrei's—for good. We're at the Solstice Lodge in West Palm Beach. Let me get you some aspirin for your head. You stay in bed."

"Okay," I said. Then I remembered the glass of wine Andrei had offered me. I couldn't remember anything after the first couple sips. He'd tricked me and I could be dead if it wasn't for Dorin. He returned with the medicine and a glass of water. I swallowed the pills and drank the entire glass as Dorin put pillows behind my back and then sat on the bed next to me.

"Thank you," I said.

"For what?" Dorin asked.

"For saving my life and for taking such good care of me," I replied.

"If I hadn't dragged you to meet him this never would have happened."

"You didn't drag me to meet him. I wanted to. I chose to dive in head first, remember?" I asked as I gently stroked the side of his face. Dorin sighed and caught my hand in his and brought it to his lips to kiss tenderly.

"Don't feel guilty about anything. I should have been more careful. You warned me that he had a bag of tricks and I still drank the wine he gave me last night."

Dorin was silent. He still had my hand in his. Finally, he spoke. "I just don't want to ever put you at risk again. I couldn't take it if something happened to you because of me."

"We're in this together, Dorin. I'm not going anywhere and if something happens, it will be my own fault. Let's talk about something else shall we? No more talk of guilt."

"Well, I do have one more thing I feel guilty about. I kind of took advantage of you last night," Dorin said. The words puzzled me.

"You see, once we came to the room, you wanted to—uh, be intimate. I refused, since you were in the state you were in, and well, you persisted so we made a deal."

"What deal was that?" I asked.

"I had to sign some papers at the desk, and I told you that you'd probably be asleep when I returned, so you bet that you'd be awake. The deal was if you were awake, we'd do whatever you wanted to do, and if you were asleep you'd tell me about the most embarrassing moment in your life. When I returned, you were fast asleep," he said with a grin.

I picked up a pillow and threw it at Dorin playfully. "You did take advantage of me!"

"Yes, but not in the worst way possible."

"You get points for that, but you still took advantage of me. Whose idea was it to use that as a wager?"

"Yours. Everything was your idea, I merely agreed to it."

"I think last night was my most embarrassing moment. Throwing myself at you while high? Jeez."

"Doesn't count. That wasn't really your fault and I witnessed that one. You don't even remember it."

"Right, so you could be just saying I did that to get me to answer your question," I replied.

"Yes, but you must know the truth about everything if we're to break the curse, remember?"

"Alright, alright. I'll tell you. You won. Although, I'm not sure it was fair. You deserve something for saving my life. So, in your research did you learn about modern graduation ceremonies?"

"Yes. I learned about Romanian and American graduation ceremonies. Are we talking high school or college?"

"High school. It seems like there's always that one person who trips and falls during the ceremony, no matter what school you go to."

"Did you trip and fall?" Dorin asked.

"No, but the person behind me did. They grabbed my robe for support. It was an unusually hot day, so my friends and I decided to only wear a bra and panties under our robes. When the guy behind me tripped and grabbed my flimsy robe, it ripped. There I was, standing with my diploma wearing only my cap, bra, and panties with my robe around my ankles in front of the entire school and their parents," I said. My cheeks warmed.

Dorin smiled, "What was the reaction?"

"Most of the women gasped. Most of the men whistled and hollered. I was mortified. I was quick to cover up, but it was the talk of the after party—the valedictorian who was pretty much naked on stage."

"Valedictorian? That's quite an honor. Why didn't you mention that before?" Dorin asked.

"I guess I figured most people would remember me as the girl who was pretty much naked in front of everyone she knows. The fact that I was valedictorian was lost after that."

"Well, I think you're amazing for handling it so gracefully. Most would have skipped the after party, but you put on a brave face and went to it. You tried to enjoy yourself after all you'd been through that day. That speaks wonders for your character," Dorin said as he pulled me closer to him.

"Thank you," I replied. I let my head rest on his shoulder while the medicine kicked in and dampened my headache.

CHAPTER EIGHTEEN

Dorin

"Are you hungry?" I asked Aila.

"Yes, breakfast sounds nice."

"What would you like?"

"Maybe just some eggs and toast," she replied.

"I'll go see what I can find. Stay here and rest. Tavian and Bill are both on the lookout," I said before stepping out into the hallway.

I pulled out my cell phone and brought the Emperor's number up. He needed to know what Andrei had done. There was no answer.

Tavian approached me in the hall.

"Everything alright?" he asked.

"Aside from the headache, she's doing fine. Did you hide the archives?"

"Yes, I sent them back home with instructions for them to be taken to your new residence."

"Perfect. Keep an eye on things while I get her some breakfast, will you?"

"Of course. I'll do a perimeter check and circle back."

Tavian continued down the hall and I decided to try the Emperor again. There was still no answer.

My frustration mounted as I opted for the stairs. I checked the stairwell for people before jumping over the railing and landing on the first floor with a thump. I needed a way to take out my aggravation before I went back to Aila. I couldn't let myself turn into a monster while I was near her.

There was a beach just outside the hotel front. I ordered Aila's food from the restaurant and decided to go for a quick swim while I waited. The swim would make me thirsty, but since my drink was cut off by Tavian's call the night before, I needed to drink again.

I returned to our room with wet hair and a plate of food for Aila.

"Your hair is wet," she commented.

"I had to go for a little swim. I'm feeling a little aggravated today and I wanted to expend some of this energy."

Aila smiled at me. She was so beautiful. The thought that I could have lost her resurfaced. I needed a drink, but I had to wait until I could be sure Aila was able to hold down food.

I spent a few hours with her. Once I was confident the GHB was no longer affecting her, I decided to track down some blood.

"I'll be back soon. I'm taking Bill, but Tavian is watching," I said before kissing her goodbye.

Aila

I stood in the bathroom of the hotel room. Dorin had gone out for something to drink and Tavian was watching over me from outside. I decided to take a hot bath to relax. We hadn't heard from Andrei since the attempt on my blood. Dorin told me all about the secret he'd revealed on the car ride home and how he punched Andrei for it. As far as I was concerned, Andrei deserved a lot more than that. I pushed my anger aside. I wanted to relax.

The hotel's water ran hot, which pleased me. I tested the water with my toes then stepped in. The stress melted off me the second I was submerged. After my soak, I threw on a robe and went to find some clean clothes. Luckily, one of my bags had been in the car before the incident. I had just pulled my shirt over my jeans and was walking around barefoot when a knock came at the door.

My heart jumped at the sound.

I peered through the peephole. No one was outside. I slowly opened the door to nothing.

"Probably just some kids messing around," I said out loud, "Tavian would be here if it was something else."

"Would he?" Andrei's voice sounded from behind me. It sent chills up my spine and my heart jumped as I turned around. I wore my ring, but the dagger was 30 feet away in my purse.

"Andrei. What are you doing here? Where's Tavian?" I asked expecting him to burst through the door any second.

"He's been—disposed of," Andrei replied. He stepped closer and my ring put out a burst of energy that pushed him backward.

"That's going to have to come off," he said.

"What makes you think I'd take it off? You drugged me."

"I'm about to do a lot worse than that. Besides, I don't expect you to take it off. Boys?" Andrei said toward the bathroom. Two men emerged, they were human by the looks of them and they walked toward me, bypassing the barrier the ring had up against Andrei. They must have climbed the balcony. I stepped backward and prepared to fight. I had nowhere to go, so I had to think of something.

I stepped forward and landed my knee in the groin of the one on my left and threw my elbow at the other's nose. They both connected as the men groaned and reached for the areas I'd hit them in, but it was only a momentary distraction. The one who'd gotten hit in the nose managed to grab my wrists and turn me around before I could kick him in the groin too. I struggled against his hold and kicked out as the other approached to take off my ring. He steered clear of my flailing legs and forced the ring off my finger after a scuffle.

"Should we give her the shot?" one of them asked as Andrei came closer to me than he'd ever been before.

I stared at him with fire in my eyes and kicked him in the stomach.

He didn't even budge as he laughed.

"No. I think I want to keep her lucid for this," he said as he grabbed me by the wrist and twisted it until I cried out.

"You better go quietly, or I'll simply have to snap your neck. Got it?"

I nodded and the human released me into Andrei's controlling grasp. We left the room and went down the stairs to a waiting limo. Andrei opened the door and practically threw me into the car before stepping in himself.

"Now that I have that ring off, it should be simple to get what I want. Unfortunately, my curse prevents me from taking it. Things would be so much easier if you just kiss me right now and we can get it over with."

I remained silent and looked away from him. I wasn't going to give in. It would take a lot more than a little roughhousing to get me to let him drink my blood. I crossed my arms and looked out the window. Andrei's voice showed his amusement.

"Have it your way," he said.

The long drive back to Miami gave me time to think. I didn't know how I was going to get out of the mess I was in, but I knew Dorin had come back to the hotel by now. I hoped he would figure out what had happened to me and come looking. I couldn't rely on hope alone. There was a possibility Andrei had gotten to Dorin the same way he'd gotten to Tavian. I dared not think what would happen if that were the case. We left the hotel abruptly, which told me Dorin was still alive. After all, he needed both of us to break the curse.

Once we arrived at Andrei's estate in Miami, Andrei grabbed my wrist again and pulled me out of the car and into the house. He led me to his bedroom and threw me on the bed. I looked around for anything I could use to help me, but he'd obviously thought ahead. He approached the bookcase and flipped a switch behind a book. It opened up to a hidden staircase leading down. He turned back to me. His eyes were dark and appraising.

"You know, there's more I want from you than just blood, and I don't need a kiss to take that," he said as he pulled off his jacket and loosened his tie.

I tried to scramble to my knees. Running was my only option. I watched his movements as he stepped closer and closer. He was smiling an evil smile. He liked seeing me scared, alone, and without hope. I was on my hands and knees, backing slowly off the bed, afraid to move too quickly in the presence of the creature.

In the blink of an eye, he was on the bed with his hand around my wrist. He quickly pulled me closer to him and threw me down on the bed again. He sat over me and pinned me down by my wrists.

"My dilemma is this: Blood and sex go hand-in-hand for me," he whispered into my ear. I squirmed, but it was no use. "It would be a waste if I couldn't have my full fantasy, don't you think?"

I spat in his face and he smiled again. He put both wrists in one of his hands as he wiped away my saliva with the other. He then reached around to his pocket and pulled out my ring. He twirled it around his fingers and examined it closely.

"This ring is so small. Much like the finger it used to rest upon," he said. Then he closed it in his fist and crushed it to dust in his hand before gently blowing the dust all over me. I watched as the ring my grandmother made me disappeared into thin air.

I wanted to cry, but I knew it wouldn't get me anywhere. It would likely bring Andrei pleasure, so I got angry and started to buck my hips in an attempt to break free, but this just made Andrei's smile even wider. He released my wrists and took a handful of my hair. I shrieked in pain as he dragged me off the bed. I struggled to keep up with him so he wouldn't rip the hair from my head. He walked toward the staircase he'd opened and dragged me down the long flight.

We entered a room with black walls that looked like they were cut from marble, but I knew better. It was obsidian. If he wanted to, he could imprison a vampire in here. He could imprison Dorin in here.

He threw me to the floor with rough force and I looked up at him with a dare in my eyes that said do your worst.

"I don't know what you think you're doing. I am the dominant species here. I call the shots. You're here because I want you to be. I could just as easily loose interest and kill you," he explained.

"Then why don't you?" I spat.

"I want two things. I want this curse over with, and I want to enjoy your blood while I can still enjoy the taste of it. I don't want to kill you because I know you and my brother can break the curse, but I think I deserve something in return, don't you?"

"You don't deserve anything but a long walk in hell," I replied.

Andrei walked over to me and grabbed me by the throat. He forced me to stand up and pushed me against the cold, black wall. I struggled against his hold and brought my hands up to try to push his hand away. It was no use. I tried to keep breathing, but a light-headedness fogged my vision and dulled my senses. The only things I could focus on were the short gasps of air I could get and the non-existent pins and needles beginning to stab under my eyes.

"It's so entertaining to play with you," he said. He released his grip a little so I could breathe. "I could crush you in an instant, yet you still have a small amount of power over me. That shall soon change. As soon as our other guest arrives. It's going to be a waiting game."

With that, he brought my wrist up above my head and used the shackle hanging from the wall to restrain it and then the other. I kicked out at him, even though I knew it wouldn't hurt him if I landed one. He laughed some more and left me in the cold dark room. I began to lose my strength. The tears started to well up, but I pushed them back again. I had to find a way out of this. I couldn't be sure Dorin would get past the guards I saw on the way in.

CHAPTER NINETEEN

Dorin

I returned to the hotel in a fog. My thoughts bounced from one problem to the next. I didn't know how Aila and I would break the curse now that Andrei had proven he couldn't be trusted at all. I swiped my key at the door.

"Aila, I'm back. How are you feeling?" I called out. But before I even finished speaking the words, I knew something was wrong. I didn't sense her presence.

There were no signs of a struggle, but I caught a faint whiff of Andrei and possibly two human intruders.

Of course, I thought. The drudges . . .

They took her.

Tavian was nowhere to be found. I wondered if they took him too, but I didn't think it would be possible. Panic struck. She was gone. Alone with a monster and it was my fault.

I grabbed the nearest object, a side-table near the couch and threw it into the wall before leaving the room with lightning speed. I'd get her back, and then I'd kill Andrei.

Aila

After an hour of thinking and pulling on my restraints, I was startled by a sound from above. Andrei reentered the black chamber. He was carrying a small black bag about the size of a bowling ball. One of his followers brought in a small wooden table behind him. Once the table was in place he set the bag on it and opened it with his back turned to me. I was sure it held instruments of torture.

"I revealed a secret. Actually, I revealed two secrets. So far, I have gotten nothing in return," he said, taking out a few shiny, sharp looking things from the bag.

"The archives I was supposed to receive this morning? Gone. The promise for Dorin to join the council with me? Gone. The only thing I do have to show for my cooperation is two drudges. You met them. The ones who took the ring off your finger for me," Andrei said, as he spun around to face me.

"If I can't have my archives and I can't have the council, I shall have you. One way or another."

The determination in his eyes glimmered in the faint light. He turned toward the table again and picked up a pair of scissors. He walked toward me with them, very slowly. I braced myself for what was to come. His face was right in front of mine, and his eyes turned dark with hate. The scissors inched their way closer to my neck until the cold metal made me flinch. He ran the shears down my neck, gently making his way to the v of my button up shirt.

"Hold these will you?" he asked, putting the scissors in my hand. I grabbed them firmly, although I wouldn't be able to do anything with them. He then ran his fingers the same route the scissors had gone, but he popped off the top button of my shirt, and then the next and the next until all the white buttons were strewn across the obsidian floor. My shirt came open and exposed my bra. I held the scissors tightly, but he took them back anyway. I whimpered as he cut the sleeves up their length and pulled my shirt off completely.

He was trying to freeze me into submission. The cold air of the room was no accident. I felt exposed and vulnerable, but I couldn't let myself cry. I couldn't give him the satisfaction. He asked me to hold the scissors again, but this time, I threw them on the floor, knowing they would do me no good.

"That's alright. I think I'm finished with them anyway," he said as he ran his fingers up and down my ribcage. Andrei grabbed my hips and shoved them hard against the wall. I cried out in pain as he popped the button off my jeans and tore them off. I stood in the cold room wearing only my bra and panties. The tears were coming, I knew they were, but I fought them as hard as I could.

"Oh, I'm sorry. I forgot how completely delicate you are. Are you cold? Good. Now your body temperature matches your cruel heart," he said with an evil grin as he backed away toward the table. There were a few bladed instruments on it. He took one that looked like a regular scalpel and walked back over to me.

"I want to leave my mark on you. You'll never forget me. I'll make sure of it. Don't worry. I won't do anything to that pretty little face. No, I think somewhere more intimate would be appropriate," he said as he lightly ran the blade down the center of my chest and across my stomach, swerving over to the place where the bone of my hip jutted slightly outward. The pressure of the blade threatened to slice into me, until finally the blade pierced my skin as he made a two-inch long cut, right across the bone. I gasped at the pain and the warm blood trickled down my hip and then down the outside of my leg.

Andrei wiped the blade off on his shirt and lightly dragged it across the skin of my lower abdomen to the other side, where I was sure he'd repeat the cut.

Andrei smiled as he cut into me again, this time doing it quickly and making me flinch and cry out. The blood ran down the outside of my right leg now.

"You know, I can actually feel your willpower. It's very strong. I feel it because of the curse. Maybe that's why Dorin likes you so much. That has to be what pulled him in. Most women aren't so willful. Most would cave after the first cut and kiss me. I should know. I've done it before. You aren't the first to wear those shackles." The thought of him doing this to other women made me sick.

"I'm going to give you another chance before I slide this blade across one of your ribs. What do you say?"

"Go to hell."

"Couldn't you come up with something more original?" Andrei asked before he made a quick cut along the line of the lowest rib on my right side.

I gasped and fought back more tears. Suddenly, the door opened, and in walked Dorin flanked by two of Andrei's guards who were holding obsidian daggers. His face went still and his eyes widened when he saw me chained to the wall with blood running down my body.

"Dorin!" I yelled.

"Aila, it's going to be okay. We're going to get out of this. Andrei, what have you done? You are going to kill her!"

"Relax. They're just flesh wounds. She won't die from them," he replied. At the same time, he brought the scalpel closer to my neck—silently telling everyone in the room he'd kill me if Dorin tried anything.

Dorin stepped closer. The vampire guards stopped him with their blades. I longed for his touch. I wanted to be free of my restraints, run into his arms and leave everything behind. I could see the sorrow on his face. He blamed himself for the whole situation.

"Here's how this is going to work, Aila. Either you kiss me and let me drink from you—and reveal the last piece of the puzzle, or I kill Dorin. What is it going to be?" Andrei asked.

"Don't do it Aila. If he kills me he'll never break the curse."

"Actually, if I reveal the last piece of the puzzle and break the curse before I kill you, it will all work out for me," Andrei said.

"How do you know she loves me yet?" Dorin asked.

"Good question. Let's put it to the test, shall we?" Andrei motioned to the guards. One pressed an obsidian blade into Dorin's shoulder and was close to breaking his skin.

"After all, if she doesn't love you by now then I might as well just kill you both because the spell won't be broken anytime soon. You two have been through so much already. How could she not love you after you saved her from me the other night?"

Andrei motioned again and the guard pushed the obsidian into Dorin's shoulder as he yelled out with pain. The vampire guard twisted the blade deeper into his shoulder.

"No!" I screamed. "Don't kill him!"

"I believe we have our answer," Andrei said.

The guard pulled the blade out of Dorin's shoulder and placed it back over his heart. Dorin shook his head, his face still wrought with pain, and said, "Don't do it, Aila."

I looked at the guards. They were ready. If I refused, Andrei would say the word and he'd be gone.

I turned my gaze to Andrei. "How do I know you'll let us go? How do I know you won't break the curse afterward and kill us both?"

"Very smart of you, my dear. Victor—the papers!"

In walked Victor with a small stack of papers. "If I sign these, I'm bound to my word by the Vampire Empire. You see, vampire contracts are special. There's no breaking them. All you need to do is agree by placing a drop of blood on the box, right there," he said, pointing.

I knew all about contracts. There were ways to hide things in them. It had always been my job to find hidden things like that. If I read through them, I could make my decision.

"I want to read them first," I said.

"Really? No one ever reads them. Alright, very well. Victor, show them to her. Let her read them. Good thing it's not a long contract," Andrei stated.

"Aila, don't," Dorin said with pleading eyes. His wound was healing, but they could easily hurt him again.

"I can do this," I said. I read through them with my quick eye. They were handwritten so it took me a little longer than normal, but I looked to Andrei and said, "If you add a no sex clause, it's a deal. You and I will not be doing anything of the sort. You get my blood, you get to stay awake for the next hundred years, you get the archives, and you get to serve on the council. We get the last secret, our freedom, and your word that you will never do anything like this again—to anyone."

Andrei seemed to think it over a moment. He sighed, "I'm never allowed to have fun, but it's better than nothing. Alright, Victor, put it on there and let's get this show going."

Victor wrote in the amendment and I read it over before agreeing. Andrei put a drop of his venom on the contract, then pricked my finger and I pressed it to the paper. Dorin's face sunk. He looked at me and mouthed, I'm sorry. He then closed his eyes as Andrei walked toward me with the look of victory in his eyes.

"Are you going to release me?" I asked.

"No, I think I'll keep you restrained for this. I like the aesthetic of it. Let's just call it even for the no sex clause."

I glared at him as he brought his face close to mine. I had to kiss him, but I hadn't anticipated how difficult it would really be. I slowly brought my lips to his and kissed him. He immediately took over and pressed his mouth harshly into mine. He parted my lips with his tongue. I fought to keep him out of my mouth. Then, just as quickly as he'd taken over, he moved his lips to my neck and bit in. I felt a rush of pain, followed by the sense of blood flowing out of the wounds he'd created with his sharp teeth. A tingling sensation came to my fingertips and toes and then reached my wrists. He was taking too much blood.

Dorin yelled from behind him, "You're going to kill her!"

Andrei stopped and turned toward Dorin. Then he turned back to me with blood dripping from his lips and said, "One last taste."

He bent down and began to lick some blood from the cut on my rib.

Now that Andrei was distracted and nowhere near my neck, Dorin took the opportunity—with his wound fully healed—to take out the two guards and Victor with their own blades. It was a blur to me and then, just before I passed out,

Andrei was forced off of me. I didn't know if it was Dorin or the contract kicking into gear that forced him away. All I knew was that it was over.

A few minutes, later—I assumed—I woke to the sight of Andrei's blood stained lips and Dorin's worried eyes. I was in Dorin's arms and finally free of my restraints. I was light headed.

"See, she's fine," Andrei said.

"Aila, are you okay?" he asked. I nodded lightly and tried to keep my eyes open.

"You killed them all!" Andrei said as he turned away. "The guards I could handle, but Victor? He was so useful! Now I have to find another student to train. It will take months for him to become of any use!"

"You killed Tavian and damn near killed Aila, I think you can handle me killing your assistant and guards! You're lucky I can't kill you yet!" Dorin yelled.

Andrei wiped the blood from his face. "It was all worth it. She has the most delicious blood I ever tasted. You should have a taste while she's still bleeding," he added.

"I want to kill you so badly right now," Dorin replied through clenched teeth. Then he faced me with a gentle voice, "Aila, I can't believe you did that. You could have been killed trying to save me!"

"You would have done the same," I answered. "Now, Andrei. Tell us your last secret so I can leave and never see your face again."

CHAPTER TWENTY

Dorin

Andrei sauntered over to us on the floor of the obsidian room. "Alright. This is going to be the hardest thing for you to hear, Dorin. You're really going to want to kill me after this, but keep in mind the Emperor won't take it well if you do."

"Get on with it," I growled.

Andrei sighed. "I told you all those years ago a rogue vampire killed our parents. It wasn't. Emperor Bantshire killed them. I knew you'd never join the war if you found out it was him, so I lied to set you against the rogue vampires."

"You knew he killed them, yet you still fought on his side?" I replied.

"Yes. I was outside when he did it," Andrei said quietly. "He was powerful, and in order to survive I had to be on his side."

"Are there any other secrets, Andrei? What else have you been hiding?" I asked although the answer came to me before Andrei could reply.

The curse was breaking.

A new thirst flooded my senses—the craving for animal blood. The need to drink the blood of a human melted off of me.

Andrei looked at Aila with longing as the satisfaction of drinking blood died within him. The witch took away his ultimate pleasure. Now drinking blood would become a chore for him. His new hell was much deserved and I couldn't wait to watch him spiral into a hole—a hole he'd dug for himself before the curse ever began.

Aila looked at me and placed her hand on my cheek. "I told you we'd fight. We did it."

I smiled at her and kissed her eagerly. We'd broken the curse and could finally be together without worrying about being forced apart.

"I'm so glad you were right," I replied.

"How nice," Andrei said curtly, "Sorry to interrupt, but can we continue this upstairs?"

I turned to Andrei with anger in my eyes. "The only thing we'll be continuing is a feud that will last an eternity. You deceived me for too long. You almost destroyed my chance at happiness and you completely betrayed my trust. You put Aila through hell and now that the curse is broken you want to act like everything is all better? I don't think so Andrei. Aila and I are leaving. I will hold up my end of the bargain and serve on the council, but I don't want to see you anywhere but the meetings."

"That's a little cold, isn't it?" Andrei asked.

"What's cold is this woman lying half naked on the floor because of what you did!" I shouted. Aila grabbed me by the collar and pulled me closer to her.

"Blood doesn't turn into water," she whispered.

"I have turned to water in his eyes. Our blood means nothing to him if he's willing to do all this just for the taste of your blood," I replied.

Andrei overheard us and said, "I'm sorry, brother. I've been deceiving and bitter, but it's only because I was jealous of you. You were always the better soldier, the better family man, and the best at everything. I was just your older brother. Mother loved you more than she did me. Tallia put her faith in you. I always knew it would be you to break the spell and I'd end up alone."

"None of that matters, especially since I doubt your sincerity. You shouldn't have acted that way. You lead me down this path. It's all your fault. Instead of being the man who feels nothing, why didn't you try to be a better man?" I asked as I scooped Aila up off the floor.

Andrei was silent.

"You had just as much chance as I to break the curse. Instead of keeping your eyes open, you decided to do as much as you could to disrespect the whole reason she cursed us. Maybe you should think about how you got yourself in this mess and if you come to learn the real reason I was able to get past the bitterness and let Aila in, then I hope you can find it in yourself to do the same. The witch said you'd be alone, but who knows? If you change too, you might actually end up happy. Don't let the witch decide your fate. Good-bye, brother. I'll see you at the next council meeting."

I carried Aila up the stairs and to the couch, leaving Andrei behind in the obsidian room. I covered her in a blanket while I called Bill to come pick us up. Aila was weak, but she tried to smile at me as we waited for the car. I touched her cheek and kissed her lightly. The sun rose in the background.

"I'm going to make this right. I'll get you back to the hotel and we'll get you some bandages for those wounds. I'll buy you some new clothes. I'll call a doctor and we'll put all this behind us. I'll do whatever you want. I'll buy you whatever you want. I'm so sorry all of this happened. It could have been so much worse, but the fact that you had to go through all of this is just—"

Aila put her finger on my lips and said, "None of it matters, Dorin. We broke the curse and I can breathe easy knowing you're not going to sleep for a hundred years. We can be together and that's all I care about. I'd do it all again. I love you."

"I wouldn't let you do it again because I love you too," he replied.

Aila

The car arrived as the sun rose in the distance. I couldn't believe it was morning already. My time in the dungeon was much longer than I thought it had been.

Before we went back to the hotel, Dorin stopped and bought me a t-shirt and a pair of sweatpants since most my things were still at Andrei's estate.

"They aren't the most fashionable pieces, but they're comfortable and they won't rub on your cuts. We'll find you some more suitable clothes when you feel up to it."

"You don't need to do that, Dorin. I'm just glad it's all over."

We walked into the hotel room and sat on the couch together.

"There are some things we need to discuss," I said.

"I know. I have to serve on the council. It entails one long trip a year and a few one-day meetings here and there. You may need to meet the Emperor. His wife seems to be fond of you already."

"Really? She's never even met me." I said.

"Well, their story is not unlike ours, but it definitely has its own quirks. You see, most vampires find their true love in other vampires. Emperor Weatherly met his wife while she was human, back in 1851. Like me, he didn't expect to fall in love with the woman who was meant to be his prey . . . I apologize for the wording."

"It's okay. Go on." I didn't mind his little slip. The truth of our beginning only made it feel more exciting.

"She turned out to be everything he could ever hope for. She accompanied him when he overthrew the Emperor before him. In fact, she helped him out quite a bit. You see, after the war, Emperor Bantshire and Heath were not on good terms. Eventually, Bantshire had Heath locked away by none other than one of Heath's great-great nephews. Iris, Heath's Empress and wife, was set to marry that relative until Heath killed him to escape a place much like the room Andrei locked you in. Vampires have the strength to shatter obsidian, but to do so would be dangerous.

"The building was made completely of obsidian with booby-trapped locks. If he were to try to break through, the shards of obsidian would have killed him. He was rationed just enough blood to keep him alive. Exhibiting monumental strength and will, he took half a drop off the ration every day and stored them in a bottle until he collected enough to gain the strength to overpower his captor. His plan came to fruition the day Heath's nephew was going to propose to Iris after showing her his "pet."

"Once she went inside the building, Heath decided to use her to open the lock. She turned out to be quite a good actress and got them out of plenty of tough situations on his revenge tirade through England. He tried many times to let her go, but she refused. She had nothing to go back to since the man she was arranged to marry was dead and her family controlled her entire life. Heath fought his feelings, much like I did, but ultimately they ended up together."

"So, she's a vampire now?"

"Yes, but remember your promise, Aila," Dorin replied.

"We're talking about her, not me. Why did she decide to become like you?"

Dorin sighed. "Because, she thought that once she aged, their love might not be so strong. She planned to go to another vampire that helped with the overthrow if Heath wouldn't have agreed to change her. She was set on becoming a vampire to be with him forever."

"Quite a sacrifice," I replied.

"Yes, but remaining human would be another kind of sacrifice."

"There's not really another way around the whole forever thing is there?"

"Aila, you promised."

I sighed and sat back in my seat. I was disappointed that he wouldn't even entertain the idea of me being a vampire too. I couldn't help but think he was using me to break the curse and once I was dead, he'd be free. The thought hurt more than I'd imagined it would. It stabbed at my subconscious and drilled into the forefront of my mind. I let the feelings rush over me and then pushed them aside. All I could do was hope it wasn't true.

Dorin sighed again and found my hand with his.

"I know what you want. I want it too, but for selfish reasons. I can't do that to you. I didn't have a choice. It's something I wouldn't force upon anyone."

"But I want to be with you. I don't want our love to be limited."

Dorin was silent. I could tell he didn't know what to say to me. He was clearly torn between an eternal life with me and preserving my humanity. I wished there was a way to do both. At the same time, I was willing to become a vampire but afraid of what I'd become if I did.

"Let's put this on the back burner for now and talk about something else," I said, "Tell me more about the Emperor and your life as a young vampire."

"Well, Heath and I fought side-by-side in the vampire wars. He was a good soldier who efficiently took out rogues. He got on Bantshire's bad side and that ended up in a betrayal on Bantshire's part. Heath spent seven years in captivity. He took his revenge as soon as he got out. He first killed the vampire who had sold his whereabouts to the Emperor and then he went after the Emperor himself, but first he had to acquire an emerald large enough to kill him.

"The largest known emerald at the time was the Duke of Devonshire Emerald. It so happened that the emerald would be on display at the Great Exhibition in London. With Iris's help, they were able to steal it and replace it with an enchanted replica. Only Heath can see which stone is the true Duke of Devonshire Emerald. To this day, the descendants of the Duke of Devonshire still believe their emerald is authentic. They also stole the Koh-I-Noor Diamond, which he offered to Iris, first as a means of getting out on her own. When she refused to leave him for a normal life, he gave it to her as a wedding gift. Of course, everyone believes the Koh-I-Noor is safe in the crowned jewel collection, but in fact, it's in Iris's possession."

"How did they get the replicas?"

"They went to a witch who could generate a magical replica of them, then at the exhibition they created a few diversions and switched the real ones out for the replicas," Dorin explained.

"So why did they need the emerald, I thought obsidian was the only thing that could kill a vampire?" I asked.

"The Emperor and his royal family must be killed by obsidian and emerald. The two stones must be in the heart at the same time. The emerald strips the royal status and the obsidian kills the vampire. The vampire who kills the Emperor becomes the new Emperor, and if the royal family survives, they slowly revert back to normal vampires, it takes about a year before they can be killed using just obsidian."

"How is the royal family chosen?"

"The Emperor must let the vampires he wants to become his family drink his venom. His venom in their system is what makes them royal, although they're not able to make governing decisions unless he approves them. That's why it takes a while for the royal family to revert back if they aren't killed. The venom of the Emperor must be allowed to die in their system," Dorin replied.

"So he's pretty much the top dog? He decides everything in your world?"

"Yep. He deserves it too after what he went through, and he's a much better ruler than the last one. He makes sure our secret is kept. He deals with any vampires who step out of line and he makes sure all new vampires have a swami."

"What's that?" I asked.

"For the first two years of our vampire life, we must study the way of the vampire under another vampire who is approved to be a swami. I'm approved, but since I had that curse placed upon me, I haven't taken anyone under my wing, so to speak. Now that I'll be on the council and the curse is lifted, I have a feeling he'll want me to take at least one new vampire on and keep the cycle going."

The thought of having another vampire around while I was trying to spend time with Dorin was strange. I hoped Dorin wasn't chosen to be a swami. We'd been through enough without him having to invest his time in a young vampire who might also want my blood.

"So, am I going to meet the Emperor?"

"He wants to meet you, and so does his wife, so, yes. I trust them enough to introduce you. Heath doesn't drink directly from humans. He drinks from animals when he's in the mood for something fresh. Iris is the same way, although sometimes she prefers to drink human blood, but when she does she gets it from a blood bank these days."

"Really? I got the impression most vampires would rather have it straight from the source."

"Most do, but Heath ordered all vampires to be careful and there are laws on how many humans a vampire can drink from in a year. Most vampires drug their prey so they won't remember. Of course, many vampires break the rules, like Andrei. I did too, but I guess my attitude was, 'Hey, I've been asleep for a hundred years, and my blood allowance has accumulated.' Until I met you, of course. Sorry. I don't mean to make you uncomfortable."

"Don't worry about me, Dorin. I told you I accept you. That includes your past. Talking about your past doesn't make me uncomfortable. It just makes me curious. I've come to terms with everything. You paid your debt by going through what you did with your brother and you even tried to make him change."

"Well, I decided I'm going to spend the rest of my existence making it right. I'm donating to charities and I plan to do whatever I can to change. My mother would want it that way," Dorin replied.

I smiled at him with pride.

"Tomorrow, if you feel up to it, I think I'd like to arrange a meeting with the Emperor while he's still in town," he said.

"That sounds fine. I think I'll be fine, but I should rest," I said as I kissed Dorin and made my way to the bedroom. Dorin closed the curtains for me to keep the sun from bothering me and then went to the living room to make his call. I fell asleep within minutes.

CHAPTER TWENTY-ONE

Dorin

I called Heath and requested to see him the following day. Heath happily cleared his schedule to see us, and I heard Iris exclaim her excitement as well. She didn't have a lot of friends, which wasn't unusual for a vampire, but Iris had become a little lonely after all these years. The fairly recent loss of her adopted son also left her craving more companionship. I wasn't sure how I felt about Iris taking such an intense liking to Aila, but she wouldn't hurt her—certainly not like Andrei had. The most she would do is press the issue of Aila turning into a vampire. I wouldn't be able to avoid the topic for long, and since Aila knew about vampires, Heath would press the issue as well.

I checked in on Aila before calling Bill and asking him to acquire some blood for me. Bill was happy to do it since he was thirsty too. I didn't want to be farther than fifty feet from Aila after her ordeal.

As I waited, I opened a bottle of wine and enjoyed a glass. My phone rang, and my first thought was that it was Bill asking my blood preference, but it turned out to be Andrei. I hesitated before answering.

"Hello?"

"Brother! I was wondering if you'd even answer."

"I wondered the same thing, but figured I'd better see what you want," I replied flatly.

"Well, I heard about your meeting with Heath and wondered if I might tag along. I've already cleared it with him, but he wanted me to check with you," Andrei said.

News travels fast. I wondered if Andrei had a spy in Heath's staff.

"I suppose you can, but you better behave yourself, and I'm telling him what you did. I doubt there will be any punishment in it for you, but he needs to know who will be on his council."

"Fair enough. Meet you there at noon tomorrow." Andrei replied before hanging up.

"What the hell is he so cheery about?" I said, pushing the end button on my phone.

Bill called thirty seconds later, asking, "Deer or bobcat?"

"Hmm, deer I suppose. I've never had either, so I'll start with the one that's easier to get."

"Good, because I wanted the bobcat," Bill chuckled.

"Alright, I'll see you when you return. Thanks, Bill."

I hung up the phone for the fourth time and sat back to enjoy my wine when I heard Aila's panicked moans. I rushed to the bedroom in less than a second where I saw her asleep, obviously having a nightmare. I tried to gently wake her and in the process earned a smack in the face just before she came to.

"Aila, you were having a nightmare."

Her rapid breath slowed as she began to recognize her surroundings. "Yes, I was. I don't think I want to go back to sleep."

"Do you want to tell me about it?"

Aila seemed to think it over before answering. "I dreamt he was drinking from me again, and I couldn't stop him. I could see you in the background, but it was the same exact scene as before. They had daggers and were going to kill you. It's like I went back to that room."

"I had a feeling this would happen. Victims left alive usually have nightmares about their attack for a while—usually until their blood is completely replenished. It's a way of making victims think it was all just a dream," I explained as I brought Aila into my arms.

"I think I'd like to skip the nap and come out there with you. I'm so tired, but I can't have that dream again, it's too real."

"Perhaps a movie will calm you down and take your mind off of things. We'll find a nice romantic comedy to watch," I said before scooping her up, carrying her out to the living room and gently laying her on the couch.

Aila

I glanced in the mirror on the wall. "Oh. My. God. I think I better shower before we start the movie. I'm scary looking."

"You could never be scary looking," Dorin replied.

"It's strange. You can barely see the spots where Andrei bit me."

"Yes, it's another protective measure for vampires. The wounds from fangs don't stick around long."

"Weird."

"Soon you won't be able to see them at all. The other wounds, however, may scar," Dorin said.

I gave him a weak smile. I could tell he still felt bad about the incident.

"I think I better take a shower anyway, or maybe a nice hot bath."

"You stay right there, my lady, I shall ready your bath," he said with a perfect English accent, before disappearing into the bathroom. I wasn't sure which one I liked better—the Romanian accent or the English accent. After a second thought, I preferred his sultry Romanian accent. The rush of bath water running traveled to my ears. After about fifteen minutes, Dorin reappeared and announced my bath was ready.

I stood then wobbled my way a few steps before Dorin met me and carried me to the bathroom. The large claw-foot tub was full of bubbles, a white bath mat was carefully laid out on the floor along with a half dozen roses worth of red petals. A fluffy white towel and robe were neatly folded on the stand next to the tub. Roses and eucalyptus perfumed the air.

"Wow, thank you," I said looking around. Dorin let me down on the mat and took a few steps back. "Can I get you anything else?"

"Actually, would you mind staying in here with me? I feel kinda sleepy and I don't want to drown after all I've been through. I guess you could just watch me from out there with your x-ray vision, but I'd like some company right now."

"Are you sure?" Dorin asked.

"I trust you, Dorin," was all I said before I stripped down to nothing and stepped into the warm water. I sank into the bubbles and looked at Dorin's awestruck face.

"Would you like to join me? I think there's room for two."

"I probably shouldn't," Dorin replied.

"Please, join me?" I insisted.

Dorin took off his shirt, slowly revealing his perfect chest to me. He hesitated to take off his pants, but after I waved him over he stripped them off, stepped into the tub and sat opposite of me. I smiled and dipped my hair in the water to soak myself from head to toe and then proceeded to carefully wash and condition my hair. I then reached for the washcloth and soap but winced as my sore muscles sent a wave of pain up my arms.

"Would you like me to do that?" Dorin asked.

"Yes, I'd like that very much," I replied.

Dorin took the washcloth then lathered the scented soap into it until a foamy lather built up. I moved closer to him and allowed him to wash my sore neck and shoulders. He was gentle and worked his way down my arms to my legs. I turned around so he could wash my back, which he did with the same level of gentle massage, relaxing me until I leaned back against him. He kissed my wet hair and let the washcloth sink into the water as he put his arms around my stomach.

I felt a sudden urge to turn around and kiss him. I did so with deliberate moves. Dorin helped me stay steady as our lips met. I tangled my fingers into his dark wet hair. His eyes flew open as I tugged and kissed him more fervently.

"Now," I said, "I'm ready."

"You're sure?" he asked. "You've just been through a traumatic incident. I want you to be sure you aren't experiencing emotions that will make you do something you might regret later."

"Dorin, I am emotional, but this feels right. There's no reason I can't express my love and gratitude by making love to you," I replied.

Dorin caressed me as he moved his lips to my neck. He was careful to avoid the sore side and for a moment, my heartbeat jumped, but I remembered I was with Dorin. I trusted him with my life and I knew he wouldn't hurt me. If I were going to get over what happened with Andrei, I had to move on with my life.

Dorin wrapped his arms around me and with a splash, stepped out of the bathtub and carried me to the bed. Water fell from our hair and our bodies like a gentle rain, but we didn't care. He hovered above me and kissed me until I thought I'd faint from the delicious adrenaline. With the surge came relief from my sore muscles and a breathlessness I indulged in.

The kissing continued as he found his way into me. My grip on his strong arms tightened as every part of me wanted more. Finally being with him pushed me to let down my defenses and every move he made brought me satisfaction. He truly was perfect.

As I lay in his arms afterward, I kissed his chest and sighed with happiness. I was about to fall asleep with my head on his chest when a knock came at the main door.

"Bill," Dorin said.

"Oh, bringing you food?" I asked.

"Yes, and you too," he replied.

"I think we've worked up an appetite."

Dorin dressed faster than I had seen anyone dress before. He kissed me before closing the bedroom door to allow me privacy. I heard him greet Bill, and I slid out of bed to put on the fluffy white robe. I decided I deserved to be able to wear a robe even though it was only five p.m. I was suddenly starving and anxious to see what food had been provided.

"I'm not interrupting anything am I?" Bill asked when he saw me.

"Oh, no. I just got out of the bath and I didn't feel like wearing anything uncomfortable that would rub against my cuts," I replied.

"Oh, well, I brought you a salad and some grilled chicken, along with mashed potatoes."

"Thank you, that sounds wonderful," I said as I walked toward the bar-height counter, and rummaged through the plastic bags. I first found a container marked with a "C" that I thought meant chicken, but it sloshed as I picked it up. I set it down when I figured out it was blood.

"Ew, sorry," I said.

"Oh, that's mine," Bill said picking it up, "The 'C' stands for cat."

"You're drinking from a house cat?" I asked.

"No, it's bobcat blood," he replied.

"Wait. I thought you were a relatively new vampire. Only old vampires can drink animal blood. I didn't catch that earlier with everything going on," Dorin said.

"I know. It's weird, but I can. I don't know what makes me so different, but ever since I was changed I've been able to drink animal blood. My swami didn't approve, but I'd get these cravings and I'd sneak an animal or two a week," Bill replied.

Dorin looked dumbfounded before he said, "You're a shapeshifter. It's the only thing that makes sense."

"Shapeshifter? No. I never turned into an animal or anything like that. My swami told me what they were, but I'm sure I'm not one of them."

"I'm sure that you are. That would mean you could still shift if you wanted to—if you figured out how. A lot of shapeshifters go through life without even knowing they had the ability to change into an animal," Dorin replied.

Bill seemed to think it over. "Well, even if I am, I don't know how to shift."

"Maybe you should come to the meeting with the Emperor tomorrow. He can tell us where to find another shapeshifter, maybe even another vampire shifter. There's a test he can run to find out if you really are a shifter or not. It's rare, but it's the only thing that explains your ability to drink animal blood this soon—because you are essentially part-animal."

Bill shrugged. "Okay."

I smiled uneasily.

"There's so much I don't know," I said before finding my chicken and sinking my teeth into it.

CHAPTER TWENTY-TWO

Dorin

The next day, I prepared Aila for the visit to the Emperor. "They will probably want to check us for weapons. Just let them see your purse and whatever else. Usually, they have x-ray vision so they can see if we're carrying anything under our clothing."

"Great," Aila replied.

"They behave with the utmost professionalism," I said apologetically.

"It's alright. Just not looking forward to it, that's all. It's like getting on a plane, I suppose," Aila added.

Bill drove us to the Emperor's estate. Andrei was waiting and greeted us as we stepped out of the vehicle. I kept a good distance between Aila and Andrei as I eyed him with warning. We passed security and were shown once again to the back of the large house to the pool area.

Iris lounged on a seat and eating grapes. Heath played chess with a drudge.

"Checkmate," he said to the drudge.

He looked up from his game to see the four of us arrive then stood to greet us.

"Dorin! Andrei! Hello again. This must be the lovely Aila," he said offering his hand to her. She returned the gesture, shaking his hand. Iris approached.

"I'm so glad to meet you!" Iris said, giving Aila a hug. Her eyebrows arched in surprise, but after a moment, she settled.

"And who is this?" Heath said turning his attention to Bill.

"This is my driver, Bill Cromwell. I think he's an undiscovered vampire shifter. I put the pieces together last night. I'd known that he's a young vampire, but last night he told me he's been able to drink animal blood since his creation."

"How interesting!" Heath replied. "Didn't your swami make the connection?"

"No, your highness," Bill said with a bow. "He knew I drank animal blood, but did not inform me that only shape shifters turned to vampires could do this at such a young age. It was Dorin who made the connection."

"Who was your swami?" Heath asked.

"Anton DeLance, your highness," Bill replied.

"Ah, Mr. DeLance. I know him quite well. I wonder why he didn't inform you. Perhaps he meant to keep it to himself, though for what reason?"

"I'm not sure, Heath, but I know there are some tests you can run and I believe there's also a vampire shifter on the council. I was hoping we could get him proper training. He's never shifted before," I replied.

"Of course! I'll contact him right away. We must get you the training you need, you could be very useful," Heath said to Bill, then motioned to one of his drudges. "Take him to be tested for the shifting gene and then bring him back to us, please."

The drudge nodded and led Bill into the house. Attention switched back to us. We sat with Heath and Iris at one of the rounded patio tables. Aila sat between Iris and me, with Heath next to Iris and Andrei between Heath and me.

"Such a beautiful day. So, what do I owe the pleasure of this meeting? Surely the curse is not yet broken?" Heath said incredulously.

"Actually, it is," I replied. Andrei nodded.

"Amazing. You've known her for what? A little more than a week now and the two of you are already free of your curse? How was it done?"

"Andrei was keeping some secrets from me. Once they were revealed, Aila's love remained, and the curse was broken. It did, however, take a great deal of negotiating to get the secrets out of him."

Heath turned to Andrei with a questioning gaze. Andrei then admitted to what had happened. "Jealousy overtook me. I wanted something to remember the satisfaction I once had that accompanied drinking blood. Now that the curse is broken, no matter what amount of blood I drink, I don't feel the same release I used to. It's become a chore that must be carried out if I want to continue my existence. I knew it would be this way because Aila picked Dorin, of course. Seeing as how she emanated such a delectable scent, I decided I should drink her blood. Dorin didn't like that, and neither did she."

I barged in on his excuses. "He kidnapped her and forced her to allow him to drink from her. He threatened to have me killed if she didn't allow it."

Heath's eyes turned to Aila for confirmation. She nodded quietly. Heath sighed and looked back toward us.

"Why didn't you claim her as a prospect?" he asked.

"Prospect? I must have missed something, I thought that practice was outlawed years ago," I replied.

"I suppose this law was re-introduced while you slept and that's why you didn't know you had the advantage of claiming her. Since you didn't, I cannot punish him. But I do believe this matter between you must be settled before you join the council, if that is your decision, of course."

"That's another matter we came to discuss. We're accepting your offer to be on the council. How do you propose we settle the matter between us?" I asked.

Andrei agreed. "Yes, what do you suggest we do to put this behind us?"

Heath smiled a sly grin. "I suppose only an infighting will do. Do you both agree?"

Andrei and I exchanged glances. I was the first to verbally agree and Andrei nodded.

"What is that?" Aila asked, turning to Iris.

Iris smiled at her.

"It's what vampires do to take out their frustrations on one another. Basically, they just kick and punch and roll around in the dirt until they get tired of it. At the end, they call a truce. They won't be seriously hurt, dear. No obsidian allowed. The practice is barbaric but harmless," she explained in her British accent.

"I'll be okay. I've done this a few times, and this definitely isn't the first time I've gone up against Andrei," I said, kissing her forehead.

"I usually win," I added with a whisper. Aila smiled an uneasy smile but she seemed like she could handle it.

Andrei and I started stripping down to our slacks. Heath was enthralled. He'd always loved a good fight.

148

"Are you sure you want us to do this here?" I asked him.

"We're getting ready to leave town anyway," Heath replied.

"The landscaping at this property is dreadful anyway," Iris added.

Andrei shrugged. "Alright! Let's do this, brother."

Aila

Dorin and Andrei stared at each other for a long moment before Dorin growled and barreled into Andrei with a loud crash through a bush. They rolled into the middle of the courtyard, taking out bushes and flower beds in the process. Dorin ended up underneath Andrei, but quickly kicked him which made Andrei fly backward into the air, crashing into the tool shed and taking out most of the wall. He promptly regained his footing then barreled into Dorin, punching him and earning a few punches in return.

Heath and Iris seemed to be entertained by it. I winced with each punch and a flashback to my dream washed over me.

The fight went on for about 20 minutes before they finally stopped and shook hands.

Dorin was the clear winner, with less bruising than Andrei, which I was thankful for. Their slacks, however, were ruined and dirt was caked onto their skin.

"Go ahead and use the outdoor shower over there," Heath said.

Dorin and Andrei washed up and then returned. Their bruises were already healed. Seeing Dorin all wet again reminded me of the previous night. I shook the image from my mind, I had to concentrate. We were at business meeting, or at the very least an important meeting.

"Alright. So, now that the two of you got all your rage out, can we proceed with the discussion of your joining the council?"

"Yes," they said in unison.

"Alright. First thing is first, I should tell you who you are to replace. That will be Charles Van Shelton and Howard Sanford. Dorin, you'll take over Charles' territory and Andrei you'll take Howard's. That leaves Dorin with Europe and Andrei with North America, I thought it fitting since Dorin prefers to live in Romania and Andrei prefers to live here. Our first full council meeting introducing you two as members will be on July 1st. Invitations will be sent out a month prior."

Dorin and Andrei nodded.

"This will also be the date of your initiation ceremony, however, I . . . resolved . . . my issues with Charles and Howard, and so starting today, you are both acting council members. Congrats, men!"

"Thank you, Heath. I'm so glad to be free of that damned curse and finally able to serve you as I wanted for many years," Andrei said.

"I'm honored to serve you as well and I plan to do my best as a council member," Dorin added.

"I'm happy to welcome the two of you. Thanks to Aila, I feel my council is finally at its best, which brings us to the next matter at hand. Dorin, when are you planning to turn her?"

Dorin's body tensed at the question. I reached over with my hand to hold his. He took a tight hold on it and said, "I'm not entirely sure. We haven't talked about it, really."

The Emperor turned to me and asked, "How do you feel about becoming a vampire?"

I glanced at Dorin. He'd told me to be honest when answering questions for the Emperor, so I told him, "I feel ready."

Dorin closed his eyes and sighed while Heath and Iris seemed amused. Iris was likely happy to have someone to talk to and Heath glad another human would join the ranks of the vampire world. Dorin dreaded me becoming a vampire, but it was the only way we could truly be happy.

"Dorin. Andrei. I have a surprise for you. And you too, Aila." He motioned to one of the drudges who had been waiting for his command and immediately disappeared into the house.

A few moments later, he came back with a woman trailing behind him. She was tall and slender with dark black hair and pale skin. Her eyes were bright blue, much like mine. She wore black from head to toe, which was strange for this time of year and strange for Florida. My first thought was that she was another vampire, with her pale skin, but I quickly decided she wasn't. I looked to Dorin who immediately went rigid as recognition overtook his face. Deep down I knew who the woman was, but I'd thought it impossible.

"Hello, boys," the woman said in her smooth voice. Andrei and Dorin didn't answer her, they were both simply awestruck and still as deer standing in the road with headlights ablaze in their eyes.

"You remember Tallia. She unlocked the path to the witch's immortality and she heard about you trying to break her curse. She's here to offer you both something," Heath explained.

"I want nothing from her," Andrei said, turning away.

"Maybe you should hear my words before you decide, Andrei Dimir," Tallia said.

Intimidation stunned me into a less-confident version of myself. She was beautiful and she had a past with Dorin. I was sure she'd loved him, perhaps almost as much as I love him. I squeezed Dorin's hand and he squeezed back, indicating he was still aware of my existence.

"Let's hear it, Tallia," Dorin said.

"Since you have done so well, Dorin, I am prepared to offer Aila the power of the moonstone. If you change her, she will be able to drink animal blood if she wishes. Her first drink must be human, but after the initial drink of human blood, she will be able to drink from animals once I perform the spell. Let it be known that this is not an easy spell for me to cast, and I can only cast it for one in my lifetime.

"Andrei, I am disappointed in your actions against Aila and Dorin. You're lucky nothing of the sort happened after the spell was broken or you would be a statue by now. I am willing to offer you satisfaction in drinking animal blood. If you accept this, you are also accepting a truce between us. I have been in hiding for the last three years and I no longer wish to wonder when you will come after me."

Silence put us all into a standstill. No one at the table moved for a few moments. I turned to Dorin and assessed his emotions. He seemed to be doing the same with me. I gave him a slight nod and he returned it before standing to face Tallia.

"Tallia, we will accept this gift from you as you are so kind to give it. Thank you for changing my life and allowing me to find Aila. I wish to turn her, should she still agree to it, and on her night of becoming a vampire I would appreciate beyond words if you were to cast your moonstone spell."

Dorin then turned to Andrei and said, "Brother, should you take this gift, I believe you will be at peace. Some satisfaction is better than none at all. I realize you're adverse to the lifestyle of those who drink from animals, but I wish you would take this gift and end your misery."

The anger in Andrei's eyes was directed at Tallia when he said, "I made it thus far with your curse and I will bear the repercussions of it for an eternity. I do not need your gift. I will continue to drink as I wish even though I shall not be content. You offer this in hopes that I will stop drinking from humans. Silly witches. You're all too fond of humans."

Heath stood and used a deep voice. "Andrei, you will stop this foolishness. Tallia is a valuable asset to this empire and you shall treat her with respect. As for the gift she is offering, I will not force you to take it, but I do advise you to be wise before you make your final decision. You have no idea how convenient it is to be able to drink from animals, do you? Think this over before you make a mistake that could land you back in the loner circle. I will not have a council member that shows disrespect for someone who has helped the empire in so many ways."

"I meant no disrespect to the empire, I merely wanted to say that I do not wish to receive a gift from the woman who has brought so much disappointment to my life, but if you believe this will make me become a better member of the council then I am obligated to accept it," Andrei replied, bowing his head slightly.

"Good," the Emperor said. He sat back down and leaned back in his chair. "After we finish our meeting the two of you can make arrangements, and Dorin, when you change Aila, be sure to meet with Tallia soon after. Now that we have that taken care of, I think we can put business aside for now."

The rest of the afternoon was full of conversation. I began to feel comfortable around Heath and his wife. Iris and I seemed to have a lot in common. We had both been only children whose parents expected certain things of us. Iris's parents expected her to marry a rich man and mine expected me to get rich by becoming a CEO. We'd each fallen in love with a vampire who was less than perfect, but able to overcome and make a future for themselves.

Dorin, Andrei, and Heath seemed to have their own conversations while Iris and I enjoyed our girl talk. Tallia returned to the interior of the house. Her presence proved to be quite awkward after Andrei's outburst.

After a while, Heath decided to introduce Dorin and Andrei to a project the council was working on and we opted to remain by the pool.

"So, when you decided you wanted to be with him, you decided you were going to become a vampire?" I asked Iris.

"Yes. It seems the notions came simultaneously. Once I knew I couldn't part with him, I knew I had to be like him for our love to fully blossom. You aren't having second thoughts are you?"

"No, just the opposite. I think I loved Dorin before he told me what he was. Once I found out he was a vampire, I didn't care. Then I thought the only logical way for us to be together was for me to become one too, and that thought didn't bother me at all. At first, he didn't want me to talk about it. Until today, he was still uncomfortable with the idea, but I think Tallia helped by giving me the chance to skip all the craziness that comes with feeding on humans. I'm not sure I could do that part."

"Yes, it's very uncomfortable at first. I'm compassionate with the humans as well. My first hundred years I decided to hunt men who were criminals, ones who had committed murders and rapes. I felt I was helping more than I was hurting. Surprisingly there isn't a shortage of men like that. When you feed directly from a human and drain them you only have to do it once a week or so. If you only drink a pint of blood when you feed you'll drink about every other day," Iris explained.

"Does it hurt to change?"

"No, but you feel really sick. The only part that hurts is the initial bite—but you felt that pain already. That's another thing we have in common. We both felt the bite of a vampire well before being changed," she said as she glanced to Heath.

"The change can take anywhere from half an hour to three hours. Once you start the process you must drink at least a pint or so of human blood to keep from dying. After the bite, you become weak and cold. Once you drink the blood you start to feel better until the change is complete and you're a whole new person who can do things you never thought possible."

"I can handle the bite. I think I can handle the rest of it too. Drinking human blood will be the interesting part."

"You'll crave it as soon as the venom enters your system. I'm sure Dorin will have a humane way of giving you your first meal. However, my first meal was a man who had helped Heath's nephew betray him. We shared him. It might seem silly, but it was almost romantic."

We giggled and sighed. Our worlds were different for now, but soon I would join the ranks of the vampires. I wondered what my parents would say. I hadn't even talked to them since I left New York, but that wasn't unusual. My best friend might be wondering what I'd been up to, but lately, Carmen had been caught up in married life and raising her first child.

"You know, I haven't even talked to anyone from home since all of this started. My family and friends all think I'm just enjoying my vacation," I said to Iris, and we burst into laughter again as the men came back to the patio table.

"Well, you two seem to be getting along swimmingly," Heath said.

"Yes, we were just discussing that Aila has completely forgotten about her human life already!" Iris replied.

I started to laugh at the thought of all I'd done since I left New York. My parents had no idea I was about to change my life completely—that it had already changed completely. They'd never be aware of what I was destined to become.

"Aila, you say you're in the corporate game, right?" Heath asked.

"Yes, I am"

"What is it that you do?" he asked.

"I negotiate contracts between my company and others. I went through some law school, so I know how to read a contract and pick out the underhanded kinks and negotiate changes alongside our company lawyer."

Dorin sat next to me as I explained and he held my hand. He seemed to know what the Emperor was driving at.

"Well, that could be useful to me in the Psytech Company. We're trying to expand and contracts will be important to the expansion. How would you like a position once you're changed?" he offered.

"I think that's something I should seriously consider. I'll have to think it over of course, and I'll let you know once I put in my two weeks. I guess I'll have quite a bit of free time once I turn, but I don't want to work 24 hours a day."

"Oh no, nothing like that. In fact, you'll be more of an adviser. One step down from a council member. You'll oversee negotiations and write up contract templates to be used for different business transactions."

"That sounds nice. I'll certainly give you an answer within a week or so," I replied.

"Wonderful! Now, we really must stop talking business, let's drink some wine!"

The rest of the afternoon was filled with drinking and laughter. Bill returned later with Heath's drudge and confirmation that he was a vampire shifter. He had not yet been able to shift, but Heath promised he would call the council member that could train Bill to set up a meeting.

We all said our good-byes. Iris gave me a hug and told me she wanted to take me shopping while I was still on vacation.

"Oh, but soon we will have all the time in the world to shop!" she added.

I smiled and Dorin waved as we followed Bill to the car and went back to the hotel. I caught sight of Andrei and Tallia talking before we pulled away.

CHAPTER TWENTY-THREE

Dorin

Once back at the hotel, I let out a sigh. The generosity of Tallia's gift gave me some peace of mind, but the thought of turning Aila still had all my instincts screaming at me. I reclined on the couch, pulled Aila down with me, and held her in my arms.

"What are you thinking about?" I asked her.

"I was thinking about how nice Tallia was to step in and offer up her one chance at casting this spell to me. It's the chance of a lifetime, or rather, the chance of an eternity."

"You're right, but I don't want to force you into anything. I know you think you want to be a vampire, but it's not all fun and games, especially if you're going to be working for Psytech. You don't have to accept that offer either. You can do whatever you want."

"It might be perfect. I could do what I know I'm good at and try my hand at interior decorating or baking at the same time. As for becoming a vampire, I've made my decision and I want to be with you. I can handle it. I know I can. I feel like I was meant to handle it," Aila explained.

I kissed her forehead and tucked her head under my chin.

"If you're sure, then we should begin planning, but there's one more thing you must decide."

"What is that?" Aila asked.

"I think I should wait to ask you this question. I don't think it's quite appropriate right now. I think I'll ask you at dinner," I teased.

"Oh? And what are we doing for dinner tonight?"

"I've got something in mind, but I need to make a few phone calls first. Why don't you take a nap? You haven't gotten much sleep lately, I'll set your alarm for one hour and then we can get ready for dinner," I said, scooping her up and walking toward the bed.

Aila gave me a strange glance but agreed since the wine had made her tired. I tucked her in and proceeded to the first floor to make arrangements for the question I was about to ask Aila. Bill would watch out for her while I made plans. Wherever we ate, it would be private and I also had something to buy.

Something expensive that sparkled.

Something that would make her ring-less finger not so lonely.

The front desk clerk informed me there was a jewelry shop just a few blocks away and off I went.

A short while later, I returned to the room with a small box in my pocket and a phone to my ear. I made the final arrangements just as her alarm went off.

"Did you sleep well?" I asked her.

Aila

"Yes, no nightmares. Thank you for asking. So, what are we doing tonight and what on earth am I going to wear?"

"We're going out to dinner. I picked the perfect restaurant, and as far as your attire goes, I found something I think you'll like. Or at least, the saleslady at Saks Fifth Avenue said you would. I'm pretty sure I got your size right—mostly because I peeked at your dress size when we were in Jacksonville in case I would ever have the chance to buy you something like this," Dorin said as he opened the door and let Bill in. Bill was holding a plain white dress box, and on top of it, a shoe box.

"Saks Fifth Avenue? Dorin, you didn't need to do that. I could have managed with something from the gift shop," I said as I put my hands on my hips.

"I wanted to make you feel special," Dorin replied.

Bill set the boxes on the counter and excused himself to wait in the car. I went toward the boxes slowly. I moved the shoe box with the word "Valentino" printed on it. I'd admired many pairs of Valentino shoes before but never dared to buy the shoes that must have cost at least half a grand.

I then lifted the lid on the white dress box to find a Dior dress. It was a breathtaking little black dress with a low sweetheart neckline, cap sleeves, and pleating at the bust. The black material was wool and silk with textured floral designs and was the appropriate length for me. The dress had a classy aesthetic to it, which I loved. My face radiated with curiosity and gratitude.

I opened the shoebox next and almost screamed at the breathtaking shoes. They were red, patent leather pumps with four-inch heels, a peep toe, and the most amazing dramatic bow across the toes.

"Are they satisfactory?" Dorin asked.

"They're more than satisfactory. I can't believe you bought these for me. They're beautiful—the shoes and the dress—and they complement each other perfectly. How did you know my shoe size?"

"I didn't. When I got to the store, it occurred to me that you might want shoes to go with the dress, so I had Bill take a look for me while you slept," Dorin explained.

"Thank you so much. I love them!" I said, hugging Dorin with my shoes in one hand and my dress in the other.

"I'm going to get changed!" I added before disappearing into the bathroom.

CHAPTER TWENTY-FOUR

Dorin

About thirty minutes after Aila disappeared, she returned to the main room, glowing. She wore the outfit I bought for her and she looked amazing. She reminded me of the first time we went to dinner.

I took her hand and spun her around. A graceful and lively spin ended with a kiss from her to me. She never took her eyes off mine. I was lucky to have her and for the first time since the plan hatched in my head, I was nervous about the night I planned. I hadn't been so nervous since I was human.

"Shall we?" I said, leading the way to the door.

"I'd love to," she responded.

Bill waited to open our doors at the main entrance. I previously told him where to go so it would be a surprise to Aila.

We drove up the coast and stopped in front of an Oceanside restaurant called "Collianta's." They served fresh seafood among other dishes with chicken, beef and pork. It was upscale and we had it all to ourselves aside from the staff for the night.

"Are you sure they're open? The parking lot is empty," Aila said once she saw our destination.

"Oh, it's open alright," I said with a grin.

"You didn't! I knew you were a romantic, but this is too much."

"Nothing is too much for you."

Inside, the restaurant glowed with candles lit on every surface and a table was set in the center of the large dining room with roses and wine. A small string ensemble played sweet music in the background. We took our seats. I remained a perfect gentleman. I pulled out Aila's chair for her and then took my seat.

It gave me pleasure to anticipate her every need and desire.

So far, the night had gone perfectly according to plan. We were immediately served a wonderful red wine and the waiter took our order. The food was served quickly since the cooks had nothing else to do.

We spoke comfortably about different subjects, ranging from the beautiful setting I directed inside the restaurant to the view of the ocean outside the window. We spoke of our hopes and dreams.

The nervousness started to fade, but moments later it came back with a vengeance. I calmed myself with a drink of wine. Then I stood and walked to Aila before kneeling on the floor beside her. I began speaking the words I rehearsed in my head all day long.

"Aila Dacey Myles, I love you. Since meeting you, I completely changed for the better. I'm the man I was before my humanity was stripped from me. With the acceptance of a new chapter in both of our lives, I want to be the one who is bound to you in every way possible. Bound by heart and soul—as we already are, bound by mind—as we have come to be, and bound by tradition—as I wish to be. *Te iubesc, Te voi iubi mereu,* I love you, I will always love you. So, here I kneel on one knee, with this little box in one hand and your hand in the other. Aila, will you marry me?"

Aila's big blue eyes became glossy as she smiled, "Yes! Yes, of course I'll marry you, Dorin Dimir! I would be so happy to marry you," she replied as she flung herself into my arms.

Aila

"You haven't even seen the ring yet," Dorin laughed as he brought his arms around me.

I pulled back as Dorin opened the box for me. I gasped. It was gorgeous.

"Dorin, it's beautiful."

The elegant design boasted an antique style. It was exquisite. The large diamond was emerald cut and flanked by split bands that joined partway around the ring. The bands had several smaller round-cut diamonds bead set within them.

"I'm a little worried it might throw me off-balance. The sales lady lied, you didn't have to buy the largest one," I joked.

"Good thing you'll soon be indestructible," Dorin grinned and took the ring out of the box and slipped it onto my finger. I wiggled it in the light and smiled as flashes of luminescence caught my eye.

"How did you know my ring size?" I asked.

"Well, while I had your ring after our second date I fiddled with it a lot. I took the size from memory, I guessed pretty accurately, didn't I?"

"You are perfect and so is this night. I can't wait to marry you and be with you for an eternity."

"You make me the happiest man, dead or alive," Dorin grinned.

We shared a sweet and passionate kiss and then a glass of champagne. I couldn't keep my eyes off the man who would forever be mine.

CHAPTER TWENTY-FIVE

Dorin

Even after we arrived at our hotel, I never stopped being the perfect gentleman. The spark in Aila brought me joy. Our troubles were behind us and I'd finally be able to start living. I put on some music in the main room and poured a glass of wine for Aila and myself. She hadn't stopped smiling since I'd proposed, and neither had I.

The ring I bought complimented her classic style. The woman who sold it to me seemed shocked that someone would actually buy a ring of that price with no hesitation. I must have been in and out of that store in under 30 minutes.

My lovely Aila deserved nothing less than the best I could give her and I intended to spoil her for an eternity.

Heath had certainly spoiled Iris, but it wasn't the reason their love seemed so strong even after all these years. Their love made it last, and the love I felt for Aila would last forever as well.

I relaxed with her on my lap. The music in the background was sweet and low. I swept her up into my arms as I stood and gently set her down in front of me. I wrapped one arm around her lower back and my hand found hers. We danced together with grace and intimacy. The light in our eyes never faded. The dance turned into a kiss and then into something much more passionate.

We made our way to the bedroom and made love for the first time as an engaged couple.

Aila

The morning after Dorin proposed I woke in his arms.

"Did you stay in bed all night?" I asked. I imagined he was bored out of his mind if he did since the man didn't sleep.

"Yes. I wanted to hold you and keep you safe. Did you have any nightmares?"

"No, I don't think I dreamed at all. At least, nothing I can remember," I replied as I leaned in for a kiss. "Last night was too wonderful for it to be encroached upon by nightmares."

"Good. I'm glad you didn't. So, what would you like to do today?"

I thought it over for a moment. "I should probably call my family and my friend, Carmen. I need to at least tell them I met you. I don't think I'll break the news of engagement until after they meet you. If you want to meet them . . . that is."

"Of course I do, Aila. Anyone important to you is important to me. I want to meet the people who raised you and I'd like to have their blessing when we walk down the aisle," Dorin replied.

I hugged him again. "You really are perfect."

"Alright, I'm going to go give them a call. They should be up by now," I said before trying to squirm out of his grasp.

"You don't think I'll let you go without a kiss do you?" Dorin asked.

I threw my arms around him and kissed him sweetly before going to find my cell phone. Once I had it in my hands, I found my parents' number and hit 'send.'

"Hello?" my mother answered.

"Hey! It's me. I'm just calling to let you know my vacation is going really well and to see how everything is going for you guys."

"Oh, everything is going fine. Is Florida nice?"

"Yes, the weather is holding out pretty well so far. I was thinking of coming back a few days early, though. There's someone I'd like you and Dad to meet."

"Really? What's his name?" my mother asked. She'd always been interested in my love life and couldn't wait until I got married.

"Dorin Dimir," I gushed.

"That's a different name," she replied.

"He's Romanian. I met him in the hotel in Richmond. He's such a gentleman. We've gone on a date almost every night since we met. I think he's the one," I said. I fibbed a little, but she didn't need to know all the gory details.

"That's pretty serious. He wants to meet us?" she asked.

"Yes. He's excited to meet you guys and there's so much to tell you about him, but could you tell dad for me? He's always been kinda—protective—when it comes to the guys I date. I don't want him scaring Dorin off."

"Alright, dear. When do you think you'll be back?"

"I'm not sure yet. I have to talk to Dorin about it first, but probably within the next few days. Oh and I'm putting my two weeks in, Dorin's friend runs Psytech and he wants me to work for him writing contracts and negotiating. It's a better job than what I've got now and it will pay better. Dorin does some consulting for Psytech, so I'll work with him and do what I do best."

"That's wonderful. But don't you think it's moving a little too fast? You just met him."

"I know, but it seems like we've known each other for a long time. Sometimes that's how it happens. You and Dad were married within six months of meeting and you've gotten along just fine."

"I knew you'd say something like that. You got me there, but just remember it's not all going to be bliss. Your father and I went through some tough times. I'm looking forward to meeting Dorin. Call me when you get your plans lined up, we can pick you up from the airport if you need us to."

"Alright, mom. I love you and I'll see you soon. I gotta call Carmen."

I hung up the phone. I knew my mom would be happy for me. It was my father and Carmen that would be the tough ones. I sighed before dialing Carmen's number into my phone and hitting "send" again.

"Yellow?" Carmen's husband, Steve answered.

"Hey, Steve. It's Aila. Can I talk to Carmen?"

"Sure thing, here she is."

"Hello?" Carmen answered.

"Hey, it's me. What are you up to?"

"Oh, nothing. Just trying to give Carlos a bath. Steve took over, though. How's Florida?"

"Florida is amazing," Aila replied.

"Amazing? You go there every year and usually you just say it's okay. What's up?"

I smiled even though she couldn't see it. "I met someone!"

"You met someone in Florida?" Carmen asked.

"Well, actually I met him in Richmond. He was coming to Florida too. I'm in West Palm Beach with him. We've been having a great time and I think he's the one."

I heard Carmen sigh. "Are you sure? You just met him."

"I know, but it's like one of those meant-to-be things. It's fate. We're coming back in a few days and I want you to meet him."

"He's coming back to New York with you? Does he even have a job?"

"He owns a vineyard in Romania and he's a consultant for Psytech. His name is Dorin Dimir, and he's amazing."

"That's the second time you've used that word. I don't know, Aila. I'll meet him, but I can't promise to like him right away."

"I know. I'm just asking you to give him a chance," I replied.

"Alright. Well is he hot? Give me the details!"

"He's extremely hot, and he's a gentleman. The best kisser out of anyone I've ever met—by far. He's a really good winemaker and he took me to the Science Museum in Richmond. It was perfect for me since I'm such a nerd. I loved it."

"Wow, does he have a brother?" Carmen joked.

"Well, actually, yes, but they're nothing alike, so don't be filing for divorce yet," I replied with a laugh. Carmen laughed along and then there was some noise in the background that sounded like a baby crying before she abruptly hung up saying to call her when I got back to New York.

I let out a sigh. I was a little nervous, but my mother was on my side. Dorin came into the room dripping wet from his shower with a towel around his waist.

"How did it go?"

"My mom is excited to meet you and my friend wants to marry Andrei," I giggled.

"I don't get it," Dorin said.

"Here in America if one girl has a catch like you, it's common for her friends to ask if he's got a brother in hopes of finding a good guy for themselves. I told her not to file for divorce yet because you two aren't anything alike."

"That is funny," Dorin chuckled as he sat next to me on the couch and put his arm around me. "So, when do you think you'll get sick of Florida?"

"I'm not ready to share you with others quite yet. Maybe we could leave tomorrow night or the morning after?" I asked.

"That's fine with me. The Emperor left this morning so I don't have any business. Andrei is being pretty quiet since that whole Tallia thing. I think we could have today and tomorrow to ourselves. You can prepare me for meeting your loved ones."

"I don't know if all the preparation in the world can get you ready to meet Carmen. She's—opinionated. I'm sure she'll like you, but it might take some time. Let's just spend some time together and I'll tell you a little about my mom and dad and Carmen and her little family."

"Sounds good. Shall we go to the beach today?"

"I'd like that, but I need to run down to the gift shop and buy a bathing suit and a pair of shorts first. All my stuff is still at Andrei's."

"I'll need to get it from him before we leave, but for now, I'll buy you something from the gift shop, or we could go down Worth Avenue and find something and maybe buy some other clothes in the process."

"Oh, no. You are not spending any money on me today. You are on probation, mister. If we get an ice cream cone at the beach, I'm buying. If we eat lunch at a fancy restaurant, I'm buying. And my first purchase today is a bathing suit from the gift shop," I said before kissing Dorin and heading out the door in the sweat pants and shirt he'd bought me on the way back from Andrei's.

CHAPTER TWENTY-SIX

Dorin

"You do know I'm a billionaire, don't you?" I said. But she'd already left and hadn't heard me. I leaned back on the couch and decided to message Andrei about the return of Aila's things. After ten minutes, I still hadn't gotten a reply.

Soon Aila returned from her shopping trip wearing a black bikini with a blue wrap around her waist, and a pair of flip-flops. The skin-colored bandages on the three wounds Andrei had given her stuck out as a reminder of a horrible day, but it was behind us now. She twirled around with a few shopping bags in her hand and I smiled a wicked smile. She looked sexy as hell.

"I don't think I have anything to wear to the beach," I said.

"Already taken care of," Aila said as she handed me one of the bags with a grin.

I reached into the bag and pulled out a pair of black board shorts and a plain white t-shirt, along with my own pair of flip-flops. I never wore flip-flops before, but she'd gotten it all right. My size and the colors I would pick out myself.

"Alright. I know how I got your size, but how did you get mine?"

"I worked clothing retail through high school and college. I know how to guess a man's size," Aila replied.

"That reminds me—I had Bill pick this up for you. It won't replace the one your grandmother made you, but since we're going to SunFest, I need to know you're safe if we get separated," I said while handing Aila a new protective seashell ring.

She thanked me and I went to change.

After we were both in our beach clothes, we went down to the main entrance and Bill drove us to SunFest where we walked around the different events. I kept Aila close.

There were concerts and barbecues along with outdoor art galleries. There was even an abstract sand sculpture in the shape of the sun. We enjoyed our carefree evening. Andrei finally called me back and Bill was sent to collect Aila's things.

The next day was leisurely as well. Aila and I packed for our flight to New York which would leave the next morning.

Aila

I woke to the sound of Dorin's voice. I slept in for the first time in years.

"Aila, my dear, it's almost eight o'clock. We have a plane to catch," Dorin said gently. His hand rested on my shoulder.

"Good morning," I replied before pulling him in for a kiss. "What time does our flight leave?"

"Ten-thirty. We better arrive around ten, though."

"Ten? Shouldn't we get there earlier? I don't know how much experience you've had with commercial airlines, but they usually want you there at least an hour before," I said as I sat up in the bed and swung my legs off the side.

"Who said anything about commercial?" Dorin asked with a sly grin.

"Tell me you didn't hire a private jet. Dorin, really, we could just take a commercial flight. We could sit in first class if you want. Private jets are a little much, don't you think?"

"You'll have to start getting used to being engaged to a billionaire," Dorin said.

He then swept me off the bed and spun around with me, before gently letting me down and kissing my forehead. My face was frozen. I had the feeling he was wealthy, but I had no concept of how wealthy.

"Apparently, I do," I said in a shocked tone. I shook my head, "How on Earth? Never mind. Don't answer that. I don't think I want to know."

"That's what happens when you're rich and then you go to sleep for a hundred years with your money in an investors' hands—you wake up even richer," he answered anyway.

"Since we're going to be married, I feel obligated to tell you that in order to obtain this wealth, I stole quite a few things back in the day. Artwork. Gold. Rare artifacts—you name it. The black market was very good to me. But, I've decided to give back to charities and people who need it."

I was still shocked. "My fiancé. Vampire and international thief."

"I forgot to tell you about all of that. When you decided to accept my past, that must have taken it off the table for things you needed to know in order to break the curse. I'm sure the statute of limitations has run out on all of those little heists anyway."

"I hope so. I don't want to see you in prison," I replied.

Dorin laughed, "As if there's one that could hold me!"

I giggled along with him. It didn't take us long to get ready to go. Bill drove us to the airport and told us he'd be in touch. He was going to meet the vampire shifter in Jacksonville.

The small private jet worried me a little. I hadn't taken a long trip in a small plane before, but it was nice to have it to ourselves, except for the pilot and small crew.

We landed in New York a few hours later. I was happy to be home and excited to introduce Dorin to my family and friends. We opted for a cab so we could do a little shopping. Soon we arrived at my apartment to settle in shortly before our scheduled dinner with my parents.

CHAPTER TWENTY-SEVEN

Dorin

I took in the aesthetic of Aila's apartment. It was close to what I'd imagined. She decorated in a traditional style with some modern influences. Her desk took up a corner of the living room. It boasted an elegant Queen Anne style and a computer sat on its surface. The leather couch occupied the same wall as the desk. It faced the opposite wall which had a flat-screen television mounted to it.

A claw-foot chair upholstered in a pale green color sat angled near the far wall. The color complemented the room nicely and matched the long green curtains behind the desk and the couch. The entertainment center was a modern piece made to look Victorian. It was situated just below the television. A few black and white pictures of old jewelry hung on the walls of the living room.

The kitchen was much more modern and a contrast to the living room with black and white being the predominant colors and red accents popping up in small appliances and miscellaneous items.

Aila lead me to the bedroom so we could put our things down.

Silky, deep blue blankets draped her four-poster bed. Lacy black mesh adorned the canopy and a small black trunk sat at the foot of the bed. My expert eyes spotted the workmanship from a century ago.

The black bedside tables were reproductions of antique tables, painted black, and the same went for her dresser. I admired how she mixed antique and modern pieces seamlessly.

Aila showed me the bathroom, which we had passed on the way to the bedroom. The white walls and crisp ceramic tiles made it feel clean and welcoming. Accents of a soft, opaque blue that matched her eyes added a spa element.

"They wouldn't let me put in a claw-foot tub unless I bought the place. I like the apartment and all, but I didn't want to tie myself down to it when I have the ambition to do more with my dream home," Aila told me.

"I like your style," I replied, "Tell me about your dream home."

Aila and I sat down and she launched into the details of her dream home. Before long, it was time to go to her parents' house for dinner. Her mother cooked a ham along with all the fixings. I wanted to make sure I made a good impression so I bought white roses for Aila's mother. She told me her father was a fan of whiskey, so I picked up an expensive bottle before we left Florida.

Outside of her parents' townhouse, Aila rang the doorbell. I heard her mother exclaim excitedly, "They're here!" while her father grunted.

The door flew open and a happy woman pulled us inside and gave us both hugs. She looked a lot like Aila only with shorter hair turning white with age. She had the same thin frame, the same blue eyes, and the same beautiful smile.

"Good evening, Mr. and Mrs. Myles!" I said as Aila's mother pulled away from the hug she'd given me.

"These are for you," I said, holding out the roses.

"Oh, my. They're beautiful!" she exclaimed before grabbing them and hurrying off to put them in the center of the table.

Aila's father stepped forward to shake my hand. I had no doubt I could give him the most firm handshake he ever received, but I settled for a humanly firm handshake instead.

"Hello, Mr. Myles. I'm Dorin Dimir. It's nice to finally meet you. Aila told me a lot about both of you and I'm so happy to meet the people who brought this wonderful woman into the world."

"Hello, Dorin. Thank you for coming," Aila's father said plainly.

"Dad, Dorin's got something for you too," Aila said with a slight scold directed at her father.

I produced the bottle of whiskey and handed it to Aila's father. He took the bottle to examine it. He then smiled and said, "You have good taste, my boy!"

And that was all it took for me to win over Aila's father. After that, Brian and I got along well.

Aila and Kitty, as she liked to be called, finished up dinner. Kitty's real name was Katherine, but she despised the nickname Kathy and thought her full name was too proper. She insisted I call her Kitty. While dinner was being put on the table by Kitty and Aila, Brian showed me his gun collection.

"I'm not trying to scare you off or anything, you just seem like the kind of man who can appreciate this kind of stuff," Brian explained.

"I don't think you could scare me away from your daughter, sir. She's amazing, and you are correct to assume I'd enjoy seeing your expansive and impressive collection.

You've got old guns, new guns, and every kind of gun a man should have."

"Well, I was in Desert Storm, and then I was an instructor for the Marines. After that, I got into the corporate world, but guns are in my blood. My father was in WWII and his father was in WWI. How about you? Any military action?"

"Well, yes, a little. Romania is small, but we do have a military force. It's called the Romanian Armed Forces. Much like America, there are divisions consisting of land, air and naval. Our numbers are only about 90,000 strong, but we contributed to the occupation of Iraq and were one of the last countries to withdraw our troops. We also have numbers in Afghanistan. I did a tour, as you would call it, in Iraq, but when we withdrew I was able to leave the military and return to my vineyard," I replied. I didn't like lying to Aila's father, but I had no choice. I couldn't very well tell him the truth about the war I had actually been in.

"Well, it seems as though you're well-rounded. Many talents and interests—much like myself. I enjoy a good whiskey and a good wine, but another of my favorites is brandy," Brian stated.

"Did you know Romania is the world's second largest plum producer?" I asked.

"No, I had no idea. Why do you ask?"

"Well, in my vineyard I also grow plums. With those plums, I make tuiça. It is a brandy of sorts and Romania's most traditional beverage. Tonight, I believe Aila brought a bottle of it with her along with a bottle of my wine."

"Well. What are we waiting for?" Brian asked, making his way out of his room of guns and into the kitchen.

I followed and caught Aila's eye with a wink. She smiled when she saw how friendly her father was and gave me a little thumbs-up gesture.

I grinned back at her and opened the bottle of plum brandy to pour a tumbler for myself and Brian.

"I think my mom and I are going to drink wine," Aila said, reaching for the bottle.

I grabbed the bottle. "Allow me, darling."

Aila helped me carry the glasses to the table and we all sat down for the dinner Kitty had prepared.

"So, Aila tells us you're consulting for Psytech. Is that right?" Kitty asked.

"Yes. A good friend of mine owns the company, and he wanted me on to run inspections and take on a more advisory role. He's offered Aila a position as well, he always wondered who negotiated for Pallin-Trego Corporations, and when I introduced her, they got to talking. Turns out he's been looking for a good contract advisor and negotiator."

Brian seemed impressed. "She did mention a position with Psytech, but she didn't say it was so high up I hope you decide to take it Aila, I think that would be very good for you."

Aila smiled. "I decided to accept the position, I have to put in my two weeks at Pallin-Trego."

"Of course, very professional of you," Brian replied.

Kitty seemed happy with the announcement too. "Congratulations, honey!"

"A toast?" I began, the others held up their drinks. "To new beginnings!"

"To new beginnings!" the others echoed.

Aila

The rest of the night went smoothly. My father and Dorin got along quite well and my mother hinted at a fall wedding. Unknown to her—that's exactly what I wanted and was already planning in my head. I wasn't sure how things were going to work once I turned into a vampire. I thought about how relations with my parents would be difficult as the years passed and I didn't age.

Another thing that bothered me was the fact that my mother was expecting grandchildren. The fact that she'd never get them dug a pit in my stomach.

She already treated Carmen's son like her grandson, and since Carmen's parents passed away, it worked out well. Steve's parents were still around, but they lived out of state. I hoped Carmen's children would be enough for my mother.

As we said our goodbyes to my parents, we hopped back into a cab and went back to my apartment. Dorin was silent, but in a happy way, as if he was reflecting on the evening and the bonding experience with my father. I decided to break the silence once we were a few blocks away from my place.

"You and my father seemed to get along," I said.

"Yeah, we really did. We have a lot of common interests. It's like he would have been the perfect father to me."

I nodded with satisfaction. Dorin's own father had been more like Andrei, so I could imagine Dorin didn't think of him fondly.

We arrived at my building and made it inside.

Dorin continued, "It's strange because I'm technically older than he is, but he's more of a father figure. I guess I really haven't told you much about my own father. You only know what was needed to break the curse."

"Yes, but I get the sense that something is off there. I feel like Andrei was closer to your father while you were closer to your mother."

"The reason behind it is because he could be quite the tyrant. He never treated my mother with respect. Everything was his way or the highway—so to speak. I didn't like the way he ran things. He never gave my mother the capability to do things her way. Andrei was close to him because he was taught to be like him. My mother seemed to catch that and when I was born, she wanted to raise me in a loving way and teach me to be kind and fair," Dorin explained.

"So you never really had a father you could look up to, only one who seemed biased toward your brother. And Andrei never bonded with your mother, which is why he never developed a conscience like yours."

"Yes, and now that I met your father I can see what I missed out on."

I pulled him close to me on the couch and wrapped my arms around him. I was glad he bonded with my dad over dinner. He was the first man I'd brought home that my father had said more than two sentences to. And those sentences weren't, "Hurt my daughter and I'll kill you," or "Get out of my house, boy."

"Well, I guess that's one tough guy down, one tough woman to go. We have to meet Carmen, Steve, and little Collin tomorrow for lunch," I said.

"Do you think roses will butter her up?" Dorin asked.

"Actually, your best bet is getting in good with Collin. Carmen's a sucker for guys who are good with kids," I replied.

"Kids. Right. I feel like I should prepare by watching cartoons or something. Maybe I'll do that while you sleep."

I giggled. "He's not really old enough for cartoons yet. You might just want to try to make him laugh. We can pick up a toy for him. It's been a while since I've seen him but I think he's crawling pretty well. Maybe we can get him a little push toy or something."

"I'll need you to help me out on that one. I have no idea what a push toy is," Dorin said with a chuckle. I nodded my head agreement and we talked more before I fell asleep on the couch with Dorin.

CHAPTER TWENTY-EIGHT

Dorin

I moved Aila to the bed and decided to drink some of the deer blood Bill had given me to get through most or at least part of being in the city. It was in the refrigerator. I didn't like it cold so I decided to warm it up in a bowl of hot water and try it that way.

Unfortunately, it didn't help much. Stale blood was always less appetizing than fresh blood, but I drank it anyway and washed it down with a glass of wine. My cell phone rang soon after. I hurried to answer the device so as not to wake Aila.

"Hello?"

"Dorin, it's Heath. I'm calling a meeting for two weeks from now. It will be Saturday, the 20th in London. Can you make it?"

"Of course. My duties on the council take priority. I don't think I have anything planned that far ahead anyway. I'm in New York right now, with Aila. Do you want her to attend as well?"

"If she's been turned by then I'd like her to attend meetings. If she hasn't been turned you can bring her along, but she won't be included in all of the meetings. Let me know two days before so I can make arrangements as far as seating," he replied.

"Of course. My guess is she will be, but I have to talk it over with her and get her thoughts on the when, where and how. She seems eager, and I think she worries about inconveniencing Tallia, so we'll probably plan for it before Tallia leaves the country, but I've yet to touch base with her."

"She is indeed still in the U.S. and I believe she plans to remain there until the meetings or a few days before, so that should work out fine. I'll look forward to hearing from you then. Talk to you later, Dorin."

I said my goodbye and hung up the phone. I checked on Aila, who was still sound asleep. I wasn't sure what to do with my time. It would be another seven hours or so before she woke.

I caught sight of her bookshelf and decided to pick up a book. She had quite the collection of what had been deemed, "the classics." Titles like *Jane Eyre, The Count of Monte Cristo, The Time Machine, A Tale of Two Cities,* and the original Sherlock Holmes books. I picked up *The Count of Monte Cristo,* by Alexandre Dumas, pre. The first edition had been published in 1846. I had no interest in reading at that time of my life, so I never picked it up. During my year of study, I was only able to learn the synopsis in case it ever came up in conversation.

By morning, I finished the entire volume. Aila woke just as I read the last page. "Good morning!" she said.

"Bun dimi neata," I replied.

"What's that you have there?" Aila asked, coming to sit next to me.

"I just finished reading *The Count of Monte Cristo* for the first time. It's very good."

"I haven't read that in years. I forgot I had it," Aila replied. "So, do you want to go to a toy store and find something for Collin?" she asked.

"Yes, I think that would be a good idea. We can go whenever you're ready. I took a shower about an hour ago. It was difficult to put the book down, but I tore myself away for a little while," I replied.

"Alright, well, I'm going to hop in the shower and then we can go in about half an hour or forty-five minutes," Aila said as she leaned over to give me a kiss before she hurried off to the bathroom.

About two hours later we were on our way to the restaurant to meet Carmen, Steve, and Collin. Aila and I were the first to arrive, so we acquired a table and waited for the others. Soon, a dark haired woman with Hispanic features accompanied by a tall, thin man carrying a small child entered the restaurant. Collin was all smiles as they made their way to the table. Aila and I stood at their approach. Aila made the introductions.

"Carmen, Steve, this is Dorin Dimir. Dorin, this is Carmen, Steve, and little Collin Andrews," Aila waved her finger at Collin while I reached out to shake Steve and Carmen's hands. Then I took out the toy Aila and I bought and handed it to Collin.

"Here you go, little guy," I said with a smile. Collin eagerly took the small train meant to be pushed across the floor while letting out a small "toot-toot" sound. Aila had explained that loud toys were a parent's nightmare, but toys with quiet sounds made children and parents happy.

"Thank you," Carmen said with a smile, "He seems to like it already."

The five of us sat down. Collin was placed in a high chair. He was occupied by pushing the train across the table and making it sound off the little "toot-toot." We ordered and Aila started up the conversation.

"So, how have you guys been?" she asked.

"Oh, you know, working and taking care of Collin. He's starting to pull up on things and he can stand on his own for a little while. I think he'll be an early walker."

"Or an early runner," Steve added.

"How cute," Aila said turning her attention to her little "nephew" as she had claimed the honorary title of "aunt" since Carmen and Steve were both only children. He was now chewing on the train and drooling everywhere.

I smiled. "He seems very active."

"Oh, yes. We're lucky if he gets a nap in that's more than 15 minutes long," Carmen replied.

The conversation was easy from there. We talked about my work and Aila's new job she was taking. I felt I'd won over Carmen—at least enough for her to give me a chance.

Steve was pretty easy-going. He liked to hunt once fall came around. I never hunted with a gun before, but the idea seemed intriguing. I was pretty good with a rifle, so I told Steve we should go hunting together and maybe bring Brian along. He acted eager enough about the idea, saying that he never had anyone to go with. He'd gone with his father before, but now that his father was getting older, it was getting more difficult for him to walk around on hunting trips.

The girls excused themselves to the bathroom while Steve and I continued our conversation. Collin seemed to like me as he smiled and cooed every time I turned to him. As it turned out, I liked Collin too. I'd never been around children before, but Collin was inquisitive and bright eyed. He caught on to the train quickly and knew exactly how to make it sound off.

Aila

"So, what do you think?" I asked once Carmen and I entered the restroom.

"I like the accent!" Carmen said.

I rolled my eyes and smiled, "Me too, but what do you think personality-wise?"

"He's really cool. He seems to be good with kids and he and Steve are talking like old friends. He owns a vineyard? I'm expecting a bottle for my birthday and Christmas. He's good looking. I know I was skeptical at first with how quickly this is moving, but I think he's good for you. He's really into you. I just hope you're careful. It's still early and you never know when a bad side will show up. So far, I'm just glad he's making you happy."

"I think we were made for each other. Or rather, it was me who was made for him—after all, he's older," I said, blushing because Carmen wouldn't know how much older than me he was.

"Have you guys said the three words yet?" Carmen fiddled with her hair in the mirror.

I rolled my eyes a little and smiled. "Yes, we've said the three words. He's staying with me in my apartment. He's easy to live with. He's tidy, he's always in a good mood, and he's an excellent lover. I can't find anything wrong with him. He even gets along with my dad."

Carmen looked at me incredulously. "Your dad likes him?"

"They bonded over guns and whiskey." I smiled.

Back out in the lobby, we rejoined the guys who were deep in animated conversation. Dorin looked up as we approached and smiled widely at me. I smiled back to let him know the girl talk had gone well. Dorin picked up the check and we all agreed to get together again. Collin waved bye-bye and Dorin found it amusing.

"He's a smart little guy."

"They're remarkably nurturing toward him, they try to do everything right and teach him things early."

"Something crossed my mind as we were talking with them. Don't you want children?" Dorin asked.

"I thought about that too, but I want to be with you, and I think Collin is enough for me. Like I said before, he's like a nephew. Carmen and I are extremely close. They plan to have more children someday and I can live with not having any of my own. We can help take care of Collin and any other little ones they have."

"If that's what you want. I just want to make sure you're thinking of everything," Dorin replied.

"I am. You haven't clouded my judgment that much. Anyway, Carmen likes you. She warned me to be careful and she's always going to look out for me, but for the most part, you're in. I think we should announce our engagement when we return from London, what do you think?"

"That's a wonderful plan, but what will they think of your green eyes?" Dorin asked as we walked down the street.

"I'm going to have green eyes?" I asked.

"For the first two years or so, then they'll go back to blue. Although, Tallia's spell might give you your blue eyes back right away, I'm not sure how it works. I would assume the moonstone is used to accelerate your development as a vampire until you reach the maturity of those who are able to feed on animals. You may even receive the ability to see through walls like I can, but that's not a promise. It may simply accelerate the ability to drink from animals and nothing else."

"I hope so, I like my blue eyes," I replied.

Dorin stopped in the middle of the sidewalk and looked into my eyes while pulling me closer to him. He kissed me and replied, "Me too, but you'll be beautiful no matter what."

My head swirled with the kiss and I smiled back at him. I wondered what my parents and Carmen would say if I showed up with green eyes. I'd have to come up with something.

"Could I wear contacts that make my eyes look blue?"

"We could give it a try. Don't worry. We'll figure everything out."

"What about setting a date?" I asked.

"Hmm. Tomorrow?"

"Tomorrow? That's too soon, there's too much to be planned," I replied frantically.

Dorin chuckled. "I just wanted to let you know that no date is too soon for me. It's up to you, really. I may invite the Emperor and his wife, and Bill, but Andrei is definitely not invited. My side won't be full. I could invite the council, I suppose, but I'm not sure they would come—not to mention it's not a great idea to mix vampires, humans, and alcohol. So, my love, it's all up to you. You decide everything and I will pay for everything. Isn't that how the conventional American wedding goes anyway?"

"Well, some of them. I'd like you to be part of the decision-making process, though. I wish I could wear my ring right now. It means a lot to me. I'm more sentimentally attached to it than I am materially attached to it. Not wearing it is killing me," I said.

"Well, then. Let's get home so you can put it on and I can admire the way it looks on the most beautiful woman in this world and all the others," Dorin said.

"What do you mean by all the others?"

We hailed a taxi and Dorin held the car door open for me.

"That's something we can discuss once we have a lot of free time on our hands."

"Tonight?" I asked.

"As long as we have no dinner plans," Dorin replied.

"I was thinking about ordering Chinese."

"Perfect." He smiled and put his arm around me.

CHAPTER TWENTY-NINE

Dorin

The Chinese food was on its way and Aila lounged on the couch, ready for her lesson on the other worlds. I wanted to take a mental picture of her exactly as she sat. Her feet propped up on the coffee table, her plaid shorts scrunched at her hips, smooth legs bent slightly at the knee. Her plain black t-shirt hugged her body, and her beautiful, eager smile perfectly complimented her bright eyes.

Aila looked at me with curiosity. "What? Is my hair a mess?"

I glanced at her golden hair, curly and flowing down to the middle of her chest.

"No, it's perfect," I replied, closing the distance between us and running my hand down the wavy curls. They reminded me of the old-fashioned movie stars who wore their hair in polished waves. I'd watched many movies from the era during my year of study to catch up on pop culture.

"Alright, I'm ready for you to tell me about the other worlds," Aila said excitedly.

"First, there's the Mortal world—the one we're in now. Then, there's the Spirit world, where immortal spirits and special mortal spirits go once they die. There's the place humans call Heaven, where some mortal spirits go once they die and Hell, which is where the other human spirits go if they were particularly despicable. The last is called the Central world. Witches, vampires, and other beings can be banished there, but it was once a place of immortal and powerful beings. Now it's mainly abandoned and that's why it's a horrible place to be banished to. Any special being can be sent there by a powerful enough witch. It's especially a bad place for vampires since there are not many humans or animals to feed on."

"So, why didn't Tallia transport you to that world?"

"She wasn't powerful enough at the time, but I have a feeling she's been studying over the last hundred years, considering she's now immortal," I replied.

"So, what's to stop her from doing it now?"

"I think she forgives us for what we've done. Sending someone to the central world is a difficult task."

"Do you think she still loves you?"

"Possibly, but it doesn't matter. I don't love her. Not to mention, witches and vampires aren't allowed to be together. Witches are known to be volatile and Emperor Heath knows they can do horrible things when they've been hurt. Their magic can be amplified by emotion."

"That seems confusing," Aila commented.

"Magic is complicated. Anyway, that's the Central world. Next up we go to the Spirit world. Witches, Vampires, Shifters, Sirens, and other strange beings go there when they die. It's basically a never-ending world of medieval times. There are castles and things like that. It's populated by ghosts of special beings who sometimes visit this world, but they cannot do much while they're here besides scare a few humans."

"Crazy," Aila replied, "What about Heaven and Hell?"

"Heaven and Hell are actually the dream world and the nightmare world. Sometimes, a human's subconscious wanders to these in their sleep. The other night, your subconscious wandered to the nightmare world, as if it got lost while your body was asleep, that's why you had that nightmare. In the nightmare world, a being rules—you would call him the devil and his minions the demons. He can see the things that have recently scared you or traumatized you and make your subconscious relive them. I'm not sure why he does this with such accuracy for victims of vampire bites, but he does.

This is the same in the dream world. The being called God can see your hopes and dreams and project them onto your subconscious. Once a human dies, their spirits will go to one of these worlds depending on who wins the fight over your soul. If the dream king can prove you're innocent and good, your spirit goes to the dream world. If the nightmare king can prove you're not worthy of the dream world, your spirit goes to the nightmare world. They each see your subconscious mind while you sleep and, therefore, can prove one way or another who you truly are," I explained.

"Wow. That's amazing—to know the truth. Are these beings equal?"

"Yes. They don't prefer to be called God' and 'Devil,' but they are equals. The nightmare king is not a fallen angel as many would have you believe. Since the beginning of time both kings have existed. They do not fight, and they are not preparing for a great war—to my knowledge anyway. They see each other respectfully, and even though more spirits advance to the dream world, the nightmare king does not care one way or another. They simply work to keep souls separated in the afterlife, if they didn't, the afterlife would be just like it is in the Mortal world and there would be no point in an afterlife. They want the good to be rewarded and the bad to be miserable. They didn't want special beings in their worlds, so they created the spirit world for those of us who die, which is not governed by any entity."

Aila nodded in understanding.

The doorbell rang and I hopped off the couch to meet the Chinese delivery guy. After I paid him, I brought the food to the coffee table and sat back down. We each grabbed a box of food and a fork and dug in while I continued.

"The five worlds can be traversed, but it's difficult and sometimes you can't return to where you want to be. The mortal world is hard to access after you've gone to the dream world, the nightmare world, or the spirit world. It's complicated and involves magic even I have little knowledge of. Witches are the best travelers of the worlds and can comprehend the magic needed to do it."

"It all seems to make sense," Aila replied.

I smiled. "Your intelligence is comprehensive, I'm sure you'll make a great immortal. Speaking of that, when would you like to be changed?"

"I put in my two weeks, they said all they need from me is to find a successor, and I'll be home free, so I've set up interviews for Monday. Word will get out quickly and I'm sure that with a few days I'll have a suitable replacement, once my obligations to Pallin-Trego are over, I'd like to go ahead with it and hopefully be changed by the time we go to London," Aila said.

"That sounds reasonable, but are you sure you're ready? We could wait until after London or even after the wedding. It's all up to you. I don't want you to feel rushed into anything. I want you to be sure this is what you want because there's no going back," I replied, putting my hands gently on either side of Aila's face and looking deep into her eyes.

She put her hands over mine and smiled.

"I want this. I want you. There's nothing I want more than to be with you, and to fulfill that want—that need—to the fullest extent possible. I want to be like you," Aila said, closing the short distance between our lips and kissing me with enough passion, assuring me she was being completely honest.

Aila

The next week went by in a blur. I found my replacement at work and was free to sign a contract with Psytech. Dorin and I met with my parents and Carmen's family a few times over those days. Our relationship blossomed and the fact that he got along so well with my family made me all the more happy to be with him. The night before I was to be changed arrived sooner than I expected.

Dorin had called Tallia and she'd be there for the change, although in another room. Dorin wanted it to be intimate and once I drank the human blood provided for me, Tallia would come in and perform her spell. Dorin kept me busy with preparations. We would leave for London two days after my change.

I was going to be a vampire.

The thought kept going through my mind, but for some reason, I couldn't bring myself to be nervous about it. The only thing I felt was the heart-fluttering excitement.

Dorin bought me yet another dress for the occasion. Another Valentino. This one was simple compared to the one he bought me before, but I loved the clean lines of the silhouette. He wanted to buy me other things, but I told him not to. I wanted to wear the shoes he bought me for our engagement dinner. They were my favorite pair.

I also told Dorin he'd already spent his limit on jewelry for the year. Dorin smiled when I told him that and I caught a suspicious look in his eyes.

Dorin procured enough blood for my first meal. He also bought an expensive bottle of wine and a large amount of chocolate.

"Why so much chocolate?" I asked.

"Wine and chocolate curbs the thirst. The first night will be the hardest. Even after you've had your fill of blood you'll want more, this will help," he explained. "I use wine to calm me when I'm between meals, as you well know. I'm not big on chocolate, but I know you are."

I thought back to the box of chocolates he'd sent me at the hotel. He was such a romantic. I didn't think I'd ever get tired of the way he treated me like a queen.

Later that night, we made love one last time before I was no longer human. Dorin mentioned that once I was changed, the experience would be even more euphoric.

I didn't believe him since being with him was almost more than I could handle. I couldn't imagine it getting any better.

CHAPTER THIRTY

Dorin

It was almost time. Aila would be joining me in a life of immortality soon. My mind raced. I wondered what it would be like to watch her skin gradually turn pale. She'd look beautiful no matter what, but I'd never imagined how she would appear as a vampire. I knew our connection would strengthen, and the added bonus was that she wouldn't be so fragile.

Aila emerged from her bedroom wearing the little black dress I bought her and the red shoes she'd worn when she agreed to marry me. Her engagement ring shimmered in the light on her finger, and her long blond hair twisted into an elegant swirl at the back of her head. She hadn't wanted to get blood in her hair.

The human blood I procured was in a dark bottle on the tabletop and her chair was situated next to it. Wine and chocolate were ready, and the gift I bought her was wrapped in gold paper with a small gold bow on top.

Aila's quick eyes caught sight of it immediately.

"You got me a present?" she asked, half scolding. She was trying to hide her curiosity and excitement.

"Yes, and I'd like you to open it before we begin your transformation," I said, leading her to her seat and handing her the little box.

She looked up at me with a smile and then began to unwrap it. The wrapping paper fell to the floor as she opened the black box and her eyes lit up.

Aila

I pulled the necklace out of the box and examined its beauty. The pendant was a light yellow gold that hung from a delicate, matching chain. The pendant was in the shape of two "D's." The first one mirrored the other. They shared the vertical line between them, which had a column of three rubies set in it—one above the other. The chain looped behind the column and over the top of the curve on each "D."

"It's beautiful," I said, handing it to Dorin and asking him to put it on me.

He obliged and explained, "This is my symbol. It means I shall be your swami for the next two years, and this symbolizes you are my student. All new vampires must wear the symbol of their swami, and I had this custom made for you."

"I love it. Even though you already spent your limit on jewelry for the year, I'll let this one slide since I need it as a new vampire," I said. "Thank you, Dorin."

"You're welcome. Are you ready for the next part? The painful part?" Dorin asked.

I swallowed. "Yes."

"Alright," Dorin said. He moved closer and kneeled in front of my chair then handed me a glass of wine. He asked me to drink it quickly to dull the pain. I nodded my head and drank.

"You can put your arms around my neck if you'd like. Don't worry, you won't hurt me."

I interlocked my fingers at the back of his neck. I braced myself as Dorin's mouth neared my neck.

"I love you, Aila. I hope this doesn't hurt you badly. Just remember that I'm here and I won't let anything happen to you. Try to relax," he whispered into my ear.

I began to feel the effects of the wine I just drank. Then, I felt Dorin's soft kiss on my neck and after that, the sharp pain of his bite. It felt much like the one I'd gotten from Andrei, but this time, very little blood left my veins.

My arms were wrapped around Dorin's neck and I tightened my grip with each second that passed. He gently pulled his fangs out as a small drop escaped his mouth and landed on my collar bone.

Once the venom spread, I started to feel weak and my arms gradually released from Dorin. He leaned me back in the claw-foot chair and took the bottle of blood into his hands, still kneeling in front of me. He poured the blood into the empty wine glass and held it out.

"Take this when you start to feel the thirst," he said.

I stared at the blood for a long while. Eventually, the aroma reached my nose. My mouth watered. My vision went from blurry to sharp and back and forth again.

Sounds that were muffled became too loud. I could hear people in the apartment next to me—then I couldn't.

I gazed at the glass of blood and my throat dried up. I needed the blood and I took it eagerly. I brought it to my lips and sipped it like Dorin's wine. Then my thirst took over and I downed the whole thing.

Dorin refilled it quickly, and I drank the next one with little haste. I drank until every last drop of human blood was gone. My strength returned and my hearing and vision steadied.

I could see the raised texture of the refrigerator and every mark on the wood of my antique desk. I could detect every hair on Dorin's head and smell his vampire scent—something my human nose didn't pick up. It was intoxicating.

More human blood. I snapped my head to the wall I sensed it through. I wanted to tear it down and drink from my neighbor.

"Aila," Dorin said. "I know. But you mustn't. You'll hate yourself afterward. Have some of this instead."

Dorin poured the wine into the glass with a swirl of velvety bubbles.

I instantly craved it and drank the whole glass.

I wondered how Dorin resisted my blood—how he denied himself the pleasure of it. I hadn't even drank fresh blood. My mouth watered as I wondered what it would be like from the neck of a human.

Dorin handed me a piece of chocolate as well.

The chocolate. I'd never smelled chocolate like this before. Every ingredient had a distinct odor to it. I took a bite of the chocolate and then washed it down with more wine. I looked at Dorin.

"I can hear the people in the next apartment. I can hear people down the street. I can see every little detail on every surface. I can smell everything, and I can taste everything."

"It's overwhelming at first. You'll learn to control it so that it's not distracting to you. Shall I bring Tallia in?"

"Wait. Can I look at myself in the mirror first?"

"Of course. Do you think you can stand?"

I tested myself. I felt powerful.

I stood with lightning speed and startled myself.

Dorin laughed. "You'll learn to control that too."

I looked at him in wonder and worked hard at approaching the mirror that hung in my living room. I moved quickly again and almost slammed into it. Once I steadied myself, I studied my reflection. My skin was already slightly paler, and my eyes were bright green. The wounds from Dorin's fangs were already gone. I let down my hair and discovered it was smoother and tamer. I opened my mouth and tried to bring out my fangs gently, the way Dorin had the first time he showed his to me.

Instead, they extended quickly. With my new eyes, I could see their razor sharp points. I tried to control the speed at which I retracted them, but again they disappeared at lightning speed. I touched my skin. My sensitivity to touch was definitely less focused on temperature and more focused on texture. I could sense every thread woven into my dress.

I turned again with lightning speed and said, "Okay, I'm ready for Tallia."

Dorin looked at me. His jaw hung open for a moment and he eventually snapped out of it to retrieve Tallia.

I moved back to the chair at lightning speed and began to drink more wine and eat more chocolate while I waited.

Tallia and Dorin entered shortly after. Tallia carried a small burlap bag with her and she emptied the contents out on the table. There was a set of three stones. One was white; the moonstone, one was black; a chunk of obsidian and the last was a rough diamond. Tallia instructed me to stay seated and Dorin was to stand next to me.

"Do you have the animal blood?" Tallia asked.

"Yes," Dorin said as he retrieved the container from the fridge and handed it to her. Tallia then began to chant the words of her spell. The diamond and the obsidian elevated from the table and began to spin in midair.

I watched in amazement as they spun faster and faster until they intertwined and became one, dropping at high speed onto the moonstone which broke in two pieces. The two moonstone pieces elevated as Tallia said words I couldn't discern the language of. Then the moonstones spun and soon after started to disintegrate in a whirl of dust. Tallia lifted the glass of animal blood and the moonstone dust fell into it with a swirl, stirring the blood until it was well-mixed.

Tallia handed the glass to me and chanted more words. Suddenly, I caught the scent of the animal blood and it became clear that my desire to drink it was forming. Tallia motioned for me to drink, and as I did, the blood satisfied me.

CHAPTER THIRTY-ONE

Dorin

As the glass of animal blood emptied, Aila's eyes gradually turned from green to blue. They returned to their natural color, only slightly brighter. It wasn't enough for a human to notice, which came as a relief to me. I was happy to see that she'd keep those big blue eyes I fell in love with. I turned to Tallia.

"Thank you," I said.

She bowed and replied, "She may or may not develop certain abilities that come with the aging of a vampire. This spell hasn't been performed many times before, and can only be performed once by the same witch. It's been centuries since it's been performed and I am now the keeper of the spell, so I control who may see it and use it. Let me know if it has any adverse side effects, but all in all, she should be fine.

Aila stood with somewhat controlled movement and thanked Tallia herself.

Tallia nodded and replied, "Thank you, for doing what I couldn't. You gave him a second chance. You gave him back his humanity. It's the least I can do. I always had a soft spot for him, but unfortunately, I was not what he needed. You were and are. I shall see you both in London. Good-bye."

Tallia let herself out.

"I think you should look in the mirror again," I said.

Aila turned to me with lightning speed and smiled. "Why is that?"

I picked her up and carried her to the mirror, setting her down in front of it.

She saw that her eyes had returned to blue. Still smiling, she said, "Tallia is amazing!"

I nodded in agreement as I stood behind her with my arms around her, swaying back and forth.

I brought my lips to her ear and whispered, "Now, we really can be together forever."

"So what's next?"

"I think I'd like to show you what I meant when I told you about the experience of making love as a vampire," I said with a sly grin before playfully attacking her and carrying her to the bedroom.

Aila

The next few days passed as I learned to control my movements. I drank twice as much animal blood as Dorin, but he told me it was normal for a new vampire to be thirsty. I also learned to control my senses so that they weren't distracting. Listening to a conversation two blocks away no longer kept my head swirling. I tuned most of it out, but Dorin had taught me how to be alert subconsciously.

I also learned to curb my instinct to attack humans. There was one instance in the hallway of my apartment that I'm not proud of. I didn't attack a human, but I came extremely close. Dorin was able to stop me before I made the mistake of spilling blood.

We were about to hop on Dorin's private jet for London. My parents had come to say goodbye and hadn't suspected a thing. They merely noticed I seemed happier and more upbeat.

We strapped in and took off, landing in London that night. Heath and Iris greeted us once we arrived at the estate they owned where the meetings were to be held.

"Aila, you don't look changed. Your eyes are still blue. Though you smell like a vampire," Heath commented.

"My eyes were green for a while," I replied, "but Tallia's spell apparently accelerated my development as a vampire."

"Hmm, are you experiencing any other abilities?" he asked.

"No. Not that I'm aware of anyway. I can drink animal blood, but that's all so far," I said.

"Yes. Intriguing," Heath said as he smiled.

Iris giggled happily. "Oh, we are going to have so much fun! We should go shopping when they have the big council meeting. It always lasts for at least ten hours, so we'll have plenty of time. The council tends to lock themselves in during the official meetings. No one is allowed in or out. I'm allowed to sit in, but it bores me to no end. Now I have you to talk to and shop with! I'll tell Dorin to give you some money."

"That's already been taken care of," Dorin replied, taking out his wallet and handing me a piece of black metal in the shape of a credit card.

"Oh! I remember my first black Am-Ex!" Iris exclaimed.

I looked at the strange metal card in my hand. I'd seen them before, but never actually held one. In comparison to a normal plastic card it was heavy—for a human. Now that I was a vampire, I noticed the weight difference, but it still felt like a feather to me.

"Dorin, you can't be serious," I replied. "They aren't going to let me use your card."

"Take a closer look, darling. That's yours. You're officially an approved, authorized user."

I looked down and sure enough, the card read: AILA D. MYLES. I looked up in astonishment.

"Once we're married, my initials are going to be A.D.D."

Iris giggled a little and Dorin smiled. Then Iris remembered she hadn't seen my ring yet.

"Oh, my gosh! Where is your ring?" Iris asked.

I smiled, I hoped my diamond wasn't bigger than hers. I rifled through my purse. I didn't wear it on the plane. I finally pulled out the black box and slipped the ring onto my finger before hesitantly showing it off to Iris.

She exclaimed and said, "That is a beautiful ring! The diamond is almost as big as mine! Although, it's dwarfed by the Koh-I-Noor. You should see it, Aila, it's amazing. We had it re-cut. It was a much better and less wasteful cut than the number they did on the replica. I'll show you later, I think Heath's gaze is telling me it's dinner time and we all better get moving to the banquet hall."

"You're correct, dear. I don't like to keep my guests waiting. You two shall sit near us. Iris will be on my left and you, Dorin on my right with Aila next to you. Andrei is sitting next to Iris, and the rest is rather unimportant. Shall we?" he said, holding his arm out in a gentlemanly fashion.

Dorin mimicked him as Iris and I both giggled while we looped our arms around our men.

The dinner was full of talk about me and the spell that Tallia had cast. People were looking at my eyes in wonder and watching as I drank animal blood without choking on it. I blushed at every glance.

"They're all staring at me," I whispered. It was a true whisper that none of the other vampires could hear. It was another trick Dorin had taught me in the last few days.

"It's okay. They're just curious and want to know more about the spell. They all think it could be very useful. You're basically the guinea pig for the spell," Dorin whispered back.

"Great."

"They also think you're a perfect addition to the Psytech team. I heard some whispering earlier," Dorin said with reassurance in his voice and a hand rested gently on my knee.

I smiled back at him showing my new self-confidence. The rest of the dinner went well with toasts being held for various occasions and events, including Dorin and Andrei's initiation to the council and mine and Dorin's engagement.

The evening ended and we checked into our hotel room. We shared a relaxing night. Neither of us had to sleep, so our time together was endless as we talked and watched movies. We talked about wedding preparations. I had a small wedding in the Hamptons in mind. I wanted to invite my family, Carmen's family and Heath and Iris, who could debut as Dorin's best friend and his wife. Tallia was also invited as Dorin's sister, and Bill was to be Dorin's cousin.

The wedding colors were going to be dark red wine and pale green. I also knew I would have an outdoor wedding in the beginning of fall when it was cool enough to be outside, but not so cool that people would have to bundle up. I also wanted Dorin's wine featured. Dorin agreed to everything I thought of and even had a few ideas of his own. By the end of the night, I had a notebook full of our ideas.

CHAPTER THIRTY-TWO

Dorin

The day of meetings arrived. After a wonderful and relaxed night of wedding planning, Aila and I were ready to get out of the hotel room.

The first meeting was for all executives, which Aila was allowed to attend. Once everyone gathered in the meeting room, Heath took the podium and began talking about Psytech's newest projects which included gadgets for everything. He wanted a Psytech gadget in every family's house within the next five years. The new gadgets included a tool that would be installed in the vanity mirror of a bathroom that would project date, time, weather info, and any world events or personal events going on in each family.

They also talked about the push for GPS navigation being hardwired into all new automobile hardware.

Aila listened intently. I admired her focus and neat note-taking.

At the end of the slideshow, the small crowd clapped and gave a standing ovation. Aila and I made our way out of the meeting room during the break so we could stretch our legs.

We stood near the Emperor's chambers where Heath and Iris went during intermissions. I looked at Aila as we waited.

Her gaze was fixed on the room that Heath and Iris occupied. She was in a trance.

"Is everything alright, Aila?" I asked. She blinked and looked at me as if she'd forgotten I stood next to her.

She whispered, "I just saw inside the Emperor's Chambers."

I glanced around to make sure no one heard her. "How did you do it?"

"I don't know. I was just thinking about what they were doing in there and suddenly I could see inside. It was strange, like seeing sound waves," Aila replied.

"That's remarkable," I whispered. "Let's keep it quiet for now, though. I think we should tell Heath first," I explained.

Aila nodded in agreement. The next meeting commenced and we weren't able to talk to Heath and Iris before the speaker started in. Aila and I sat toward the front of the room. One of Heath's advisors talked about security and ways to maintain the barrier between Psytech and other companies. They didn't want other companies stealing their ideas or figuring out what they were doing. Psytech planned a major technological revolution. They were going to take over the market. Cell phones, computers, gadgets, GPS, and even E-readers. They would launch a new product line that would be more advanced than anything on the market now.

Aila

I wondered why they wanted so much power over the industry, and why they were going to all this trouble to dominate the market. It wasn't a bad thing, but I also didn't want to put other companies out of business. I wasn't looking to murder the economy.

I looked over at Heath who watched the advisor with a bored look on his face.

Once we have given humans the technology they crave, we'll take it back. Their submission will make for an abundance of blood.

I heard the words in my head, but they weren't mine. They sounded like Heath. Again, they came.

The pathetic humans will never see it coming. They're so reliant on technology that one day, about seven years from now, they'll wake up and it will all be gone. They will riot. More importantly, they will do anything to get it back, even if it means feeding us.

My confusion made me lose concentration. I couldn't believe what had just happened. Heath's thoughts had been projected into my mind. But what he said troubled me—or rather, what he thought. He was going to make humans give up their blood in exchange for technology, and it would take seven years. I wondered why it would be seven years.

My thoughts raced. I couldn't understand how they would even pull off something like that.

The council member was now talking about launching their own satellites into orbit around the earth. He said it would be about five years before they were able to do so. I quickly put it together. If they could get satellites up, they could also take others out with some sort of virus. If all the satellites were down, nothing would work. That's why they wanted to push satellite television, GPS in cars, and their own gadgets. The internet would be done for. The world would fall apart without satellite technology.

My concentration faltered further and more voices interrupted my thoughts. They overwhelmed me until I let out a loud gasp and clasped my hands to my head. The voices stopped.

Faces turned in my direction and the room grew silent for a moment. Dorin's hand found my shoulder as he leaned forward in concern.

I quietly apologized and the speaker continued.

The meeting adjourned shortly after and I pulled Dorin outside, where I was sure no one would be able to hear us.

"Is everything okay?" he asked.

Dorin's worried look made my words come out quickly and in hushed tones. Someone could have been in listening distance.

"Heath is planning to take over the world with this plot to sell gadgets and make everything reliant on satellite technology. They're planning to cut off the satellites in seven years and kill all technology. Humans will have to give their blood to gain access to the technology. I read Heath's mind by accident."

Dorin's face remained blank for a moment. A few emotions then washed over him. The first said he thought I was crazy, the second indicated understanding, and the last was determination.

"We have to go. I don't want that. I'm not going to be a part of it. We're going to have to stop it from happening, but first we have to get us and your family somewhere safe. We're going back to New York, now," Dorin said pulling his cell phone up to his ear.

Minutes later, we pulled up to the airport. The jet was waiting. Dorin tried to get in touch with Bill but had no luck.

"Damn it!" he said, throwing the phone down at the floor of the plane. It shattered to pieces.

I moved closer to him trying to comfort him and calm him down.

"I didn't see it coming. I guess I had my suspicions, but I didn't know he was planning this. He and Iris have changed. Something in them is different. I didn't realize it was utter hatred for humans," Dorin said.

I remained quiet. I dared not read Dorin's mind. He was so angry right now. I wasn't even sure how to do it. My own thoughts were almost too much for me to manage, let alone someone else's. I didn't want the ability.

"I had a feeling you'd develop that next. I had no idea it would happen so fast. The only vampires who have been able to read minds have been at least six hundred years old. Most vampires don't make it that far. After the wars, many of the old vampires were either wiped out or went into hiding. You may be the only one with that ability," Dorin explained.

"I don't want this. What are we going to do?"

"We're going to find somewhere to go and lay low for a while. We're taking your family and Carmen's family with us. They'll have to know what we are. We're rogue now, so it doesn't matter what rules we break. They'll be after us anyway," Dorin replied.

"I don't know if I can tell them that."

"It's the only way they'll come with us. And they must come with us. We need to go somewhere remote. Somewhere that Psytech has yet to tackle. I was thinking Canada or Alaska. I wish we could go to Romania, but they'll be expecting that and it's too risky right now. I'm sure Andrei will be on their side."

Once we landed in New York, we had a plan. Get my family and get out. We were heading to Canada on a flight to Yellowknife. Then we'd drive north so as to lose any trail we might leave behind.

We went to my parents' house first. We knocked until the door was answered. It was getting late and my parents were getting ready for bed.

"Aren't you guys supposed to be in London?" my mother asked.

"We just returned, but we all have to go. Psytech is corrupt. The owner is plotting to take over the world. We have to go to Canada and come up with a plan to stop them," I replied.

CHAPTER THIRTY-THREE

Dorin

Aila's parents seemed to look at her as if she were crazy. There was nothing I could do or say to help the situation. They would either believe her or they wouldn't.

I stood aside and let her handle it, but remained alert for any impending danger from the outside.

"I'm going to try calling Bill again," I said. Aila nodded and handed me her phone since I broke mine. She gestured to a sitting room off to the side. I kept one ear on the conversation she was having and one ear on the phone.

Aila

"What do you mean they're plotting to take over the world?" my father asked. "You mean figuratively speaking?"

"No, dad, they're actually vampires. We can prove it, but we need to get going before they send someone after us. We have to go get Carmen, Steve, and Collin too."

"Now, what are you talking about, Aila? I don't understand what's going on."

My father always needed all the facts before making decisions.

I took in a deep breath. I wasn't sure what my parents were going to think about me being a vampire, but I had to tell them if we were going to get out of New York alive.

"Okay. The CEO of Psytech is actually the Vampire Emperor. He's old friends with Dorin. Today we saw his plan to take over the world and make humans give their blood in return for technology. He's planning to cut off all communications with the satellites orbiting the earth which will kill anything that connects to them. I know this because I read his mind."

"Wait, you read his mind? Honey, do you know what you're saying? These things are impossible," my mother replied.

"They aren't impossible, mom. I know it sounds crazy, but it's all true. I have to tell you one more thing. This is going to be really hard for you to understand and even harder for you to believe. Dorin and I are vampires too, but we only drink animal blood."

My parents stared at me with their arms crossed.

I tried to use my new ability to see what they were thinking. I tried my mother first.

This whole vampire thing must be some sort of fancy corporate talk, but Brian doesn't seem any less confused than I am.

I then focused on my father.

What is going on here? She meets this guy and goes crazy? Maybe they're on drugs or something. I should go get my gun.

"Dad, I'm not on drugs, don't go get your gun," I said.

My father's head snapped up at me.

Dorin stepped quietly back into the room. He shook his head to indicate he hadn't contacted Bill yet.

"Mom, this is real. I'm a vampire, and I chose to be a vampire. Dorin and I were meant to be. There's this whole weird curse thing, but all you need to know is that there are bad vampires out there and we're the good ones. If there's anyone you're safe with, it's us. We're taking Dorin's jet to Canada for a little while and then we'll figure out how to stop Psytech. Please come with us so I know you're safe," I said, stepping closer at high speed. My parents blinked and looked at each other.

My father sighed. His military days had prepared him for just about anything.

"I'm not happy about you becoming a vampire. I'm not even completely convinced, but we can talk about that later. In the interest of keeping everyone safe in the case that this is a real threat and not some crazy concoction, I'm going to go along with it. Dorin, since we're taking a private jet, help me get those guns loaded into my SUV. Kitty, get us packed. We're going to Canada with our vampire daughter and her vampire boyfriend."

My mother was silent for a moment, but the realization hit her that there was possible danger and she jumped up and went to the bedroom to pack a few suitcases.

I followed to help her.

"I'm sorry I didn't tell you, mom. I didn't know how to tell you something like this. It's just that I feel like I was supposed to be like this. I wasn't sure you guys would understand."

"It's alright, dear. I know. I know you would never put us in danger and that you're here because you love us. I can see that it's not just regular everyday love between you two. It's something more. Had Brian been a vampire, I would have done the same thing. That's a strange thing to say. I still don't know about this vampire business, but I have to trust you. You say there's danger. We're a family and we stick together when there's danger."

I hugged my mother carefully and we finished packing. I had them packed and ready to go in five minutes flat. Everything was ready and we all headed over to Carmen's house.

I called her and gave her a heads up that we were coming. I told them to pack, but I was sure they wouldn't do anything until I explained. I'd have to streamline this one if we were to get out of there quickly.

We pulled up to Carmen's apartment and I told everyone to wait for me. I ran inside and prepared to tell Carmen and Steve what was going on.

Inside, Carmen was lazily packing. While Steve was questioning why. I rang the doorbell and Carmen jumped to answer it.

"What's going on?" Carmen asked.

"We have to go to Canada. I'm going to tell you something, and you are just going to have to believe me because there's no time for questions. Psytech is a vampire-run company, and until today I thought it was run by good vampires, but I read the mind of the Emperor and now I know that he wants to use technology to make humans give up their blood. I can read minds because I'm a vampire too and so is Dorin. Good? Okay, let's get you packed!"

I stood and started at vampire speed to get them packed. Carmen and Steve were in shock. Steve held Collin close to him.

After I closed one of the suitcases, Carmen stood after a long silence and looked into my eyes.

"Why do we have to go to Canada? You guys are the ones these vampires are after."

"Carmen, I know you aren't happy with me right now, but these vampires will hurt you just to get to me and Dorin. The Emperor thought I'd be of great use, and that was before I could read minds. He doesn't know, or least I hope he doesn't. Once he figures it out, they'll be trying to track down Dorin and me. You have to come with us, to keep your family safe. You don't have to talk to me ever again, but you have to protect your family and come to Canada with us, we can go our separate ways after that if you want to."

Silence filled the room. Carmen's thoughts raced and it was almost too difficult for me to keep up with them.

"I'm sorry I put you through this, but if I hadn't followed my heart and became a vampire, we wouldn't know about this impending danger. I know you're trying to understand, and I hope someday you guys do, but, for now, we need to get to the plane."

Carmen stood, and approached me slowly.

"I guess we have no choice. You brought this danger to us, so I hope you can make it go away. I trust you, but I can't believe you would enter this world without thinking of your friends and family. I don't know all the circumstances, but right now I just need a little space and time to figure it out. Let's go."

We all went out to the waiting vehicle and soon arrived at the airport where Dorin's private jet waited. He paid off another vampire to lead any followers elsewhere. The uneasy alliance between my loved ones from my human life and the new life I'd chosen became slightly stronger once we got in the air and came closer to our destination.

CHAPTER THIRTY-FOUR

Dorin

The group finally landed in Yellowknife, Northwest Territories, Canada. The area was the capital of the "Middle of Nowhere." We promptly procured a few vehicles and drove farther into the middle of nowhere—a cabin I had arranged under a false name near the Thelon Wildlife Sanctuary. The sanctuary would serve as a place where Aila and I could get our fill of animal blood. Plenty of large game would feed us and our human members for a long time.

Our remote cabin was well stocked. Someone would have to go to Yellowknife for supplies every few weeks, but the cabin contained five bedrooms, with three fireplaces and a large great-room. Carmen and Steve settled into one of the bedrooms along with their son, Collin. They didn't want to put him in his own room until they were sure we weren't followed.

Aila and I found a room to share and let Kitty and Brian take the master bedroom.

We were all settling in quite well, although things were still awkward between Aila and her family in the week we'd been there.

"I don't know what to do," Aila said as I embraced her.

"Maybe instead of trying to talk to them, just show them you're still you," I advised.

Aila nodded into my shoulder and then came away. She stood up straight and prepared herself. "I hope this works," she said.

Aila

I decided to cook dinner for everyone as a gesture.

With everyone at the table, I prepared myself for the uneasy silence that loomed since the plane crossed the Canadian border. As I set out the food, it seemed my family and friends kept their distance from me. Dorin gave me a look of reassurance as I glanced at him before taking my place by his side. Now that I was a vampire, I didn't have to eat human food, but in keeping up with the theme of the night, I put on a good show to try to convince my family I was still Aila.

One at a time, Aila's parents and Carmen and her family dug into the food. Collin dug in first, although most of the food went on his face instead of in his mouth. My parents were next, and then Carmen and Steve.

"So, how is the food?" I asked. Everyone nodded in approval and said things like "very good" or "delicious."

"I know things have been—different since we got here. I know it's because you don't know what to think of me. I've been working on my powers, and I learned to only read minds when I want to. I shut it off, so don't be afraid of me reading your thoughts."

There was more silence and exchanged glances around the table. My mother was the first to speak.

"Aila, we aren't afraid of you. I can see you're the same person you always were. It's just that our worlds have all been turned upside-down and we aren't quite sure how to handle it yet."

"You're exactly the same person to me—except for one thing," my father began.

"What's that, dad?"

"You're a better cook!" he exclaimed as everyone burst into laughter.

I laughed along with them. "Well, my senses are much more acute now I guess, but I wasn't that bad of a cook before, was I?"

"Horrible!" Carmen replied, "Remember when you tried to make Thanksgiving dinner two years ago? It was a disaster! Except for the store-bought pie, of course."

Even Dorin laughed with them now. My embarrassment only lasted a few seconds before I joined in reminding them all of my salty roast beef fiasco.

"Of course. Now that I don't have to eat, I can finally cook," I said.

The rest of dinner was much more easy-going than the last week had been. They all asked questions about me and Dorin they'd neglected to ask before.

It seemed everyone had forgotten about the reason we were all so far from home. We were becoming a family. My father and Dorin were still getting along splendidly, even though my father now knew the truth about him. It actually seemed to bring them closer—especially after Dorin told my father the truth about his time at war. I was happy to see them in the living room talking about guns and defense techniques.

My mother and I cleaned up after dinner while Carmen and Steve put Collin to bed. I did most of the work in very little time.

"Aila, you don't have to do everything. Slow down and let me help you," Kitty said.

"Sorry. Really, it's not a problem, I can do it all so easily now," I replied.

"I know, but sometimes it's nice just to take your time and do things casually."

I realized she was right and slowed down to human pace.

My mother gazed out to the living room and watched my dad and Dorin.

"They seem to be getting along very well, even after everything that has happened."

"Yeah, I worried you guys might not like him anymore once you found out what he was and what I am now. I was especially worried about dad, but I underestimated how much he liked Dorin."

"We can see you're happy with him, honey. He seems to bring out the light in you. The light you had before you even started dating in high school. With each heartbreak, your light dimmed just a little. Since you've been with Dorin, the light returned and might even be brighter. That's all we want for you, Aila. We want you to be happy."

"Even if it means I have to drink animal blood?"

"Yes, even if it means you have to drink animal blood. Just don't do it in front of us—that might be too much for your mother to handle."

"Okay mom, I promise, no blood drinking in front of you."

I looked at my mother for a second longer. She really was happy for me. I could tell without using my mind reading ability. I could also tell there was a hint of sadness about her, and I had an idea of why that sadness lingered.

"Mom?"

"Yes, Aila?"

"I'm sorry I won't be able to give you grandchildren like you always wanted."

"Oh, Aila. Don't worry about that. It's not your fault. We can't control who we fall in love with. I don't hold it against you. I'd rather you be with the person you love than be with someone just to give me grandchildren. You would have made a great mother, Aila, but I can see it wasn't meant to be. Your path was always leading you here. No one else would have been able to find out what Psytech was planning. It's your destiny to help stop them."

I hugged her. I couldn't believe how understanding she was being, and I knew she was right. My destiny was to fight side by side with Dorin against the Vampire Emperor. With the night drawing to a close, I had to talk to Carmen before everyone went to bed. I waited for her to finish putting Collin to sleep before I approached her.

"Hey, how was the bedtime story tonight?" I asked when Carmen emerged from her and Steve's room.

"It put both of them to sleep," Carmen replied with a smile.

"They had quite a day. Collin liked playing outside with Steve today. It was beautiful out, hopefully, the weather will hold up for a few days at least."

"Yeah, Collin is adjusting nicely to the new surroundings. I think he actually likes it better than our cramped apartment in the city. What kid wouldn't want this much space to run around in?" Carmen asked.

"How are you adjusting?" I asked with concern.

"I think I'll be fine. Steve is doing well too. He likes the outdoors, so this is perfect for him. I'm just used to the city, I guess."

"What about things between you and me? I hope you can forgive me for dragging you into all this."

"I know I was harsh before, but I don't blame you. I don't even blame Dorin. I just didn't think life would be like this— on the run with a little one. I just wanted life to be normal, you know? But, I guess I'd rather be here with you preparing for it, than walking around obliviously like the rest of the world."

I sighed. "We will stop them, Carmen. Collin will not have to grow up in a world where monsters rule, I promise you. Dorin and I will find a way to put a stop to this."

Carmen's eyes teared up and she went in for a hug. I took her into my arms.

"I hope you do. I can't stand the thought of him living in a world where evil rules. What kind of life would that be for a young boy? I've always known I would have to protect him from certain things, but this? This is just too much for a mother to bear."

"Don't worry, Carmen. You and Steve are not the only ones fighting for him. You don't have to handle this burden on your own."

"That makes me feel a little better," Carmen said with a sniffle. "Thank you."

CHAPTER THIRTY-FIVE

Dorin

Aila's parents and I were in the living room. We enjoyed lighthearted conversation while sipping on wine.

I spotted Aila and poured a glass for her, which she took happily. We were both thirsty, and the wine would only help until her parents went to bed.

"I think tomorrow we should all sit down and talk about where to go from here. We'll need to get some protective rings for everyone but Aila and me," Dorin said.

"Protective rings?" Kitty asked.

"Yeah, like the one grandma carved for me. They protect humans from vampires."

"Well I have some of those in my jewelry box," Kitty replied, "Do you think grandma knew what they were for? She was always making those things, I think I have at least eight of them."

"If she was making them, she probably knew what they were for," I explained. "To make them you have to carve them with an obsidian dagger that killed a vampire."

"Oh. Dear."

"Obsidian, huh?" Brian said.

"Yes. It's the only thing that will injure us fatally, but it has to pierce the heart," I replied.

Kitty looked to Aila and then hurried off toward her bedroom. She returned with her jewelry box and started picking through it to find the rings. She came up with eight rings and a bracelet.

"If we wear these, won't it harm you guys too?" Kitty asked.

"The rings don't harm vampires, they just make it impossible for any vampire that means you harm or any vampire you don't trust to get near you," I said.

I remembered my first meeting with Aila. The cramped elevator space seemed much tenser as the ring she once wore pushed me away.

"Aila, whatever happened to your ring like this? You used to wear it all the time," Kitty asked.

"I think I lost it. Ironically, just a few weeks before I met Dorin," she replied. Aila and I had discussed that the truth about what happened in Florida and about my original intentions should not be revealed to her parents. Not when they were so on edge.

"Everything happens for a reason," Kitty replied.

"How are these rings going to work for Collin?" Aila asked.

"That's a good question. A young one like him can't exactly wear a ring," I said.

"Maybe the bracelet?" Aila suggested.

"We can't trust him to keep it on," Kitty said. "He will probably use it more for a teething ring than a piece of jewelry. We can ask Carmen and Steve what they think tomorrow. As for me, I'm going to bed. Brian, are you ready for bed too?"

"Yep, right behind you."

Once Aila's parents were in bed, I turned to Aila and asked, "Thirsty?"

"Very," she smiled. I took her hand and led her outside to the cool Canadian air.

We both inhaled the air before saying in unison, "Caribou."

About ten minutes later we were cleaning ourselves up from our meal and heading back to the cabin. I was happy to see Aila was adjusting well to her new life much better than I'd adjusted so many years ago.

I vowed Aila would never have to follow a blood-hungry leader. Heath had changed. Or maybe it wasn't Heath that changed. It was more probable that it was me that changed. Aila helped me find my humanity again, and I would do everything in my power to keep it. The thoughts in my mind lead to only one conclusion—Emperor Heath Weatherly would have to die an eternal death. Just before we reached the cabin, Aila stopped in her tracks and peered into the night. She turned around to face the direction we just came from. I noticed the alarm on her face and turned back as well. She sniffed the air again.

"Bill? Tallia?" she said. Moments later, Bill and Tallia emerged from the thick brush.

"Aila, you've developed your talents well," Bill replied.

"How did you find us?" I asked.

"One of the airport authorities you paid off talked. The Emperor knows you're here and he plans to come soon. I found out through Tallia and had to come warn you, I know you have Aila's family with you."

"Tallia, why did you come?" was my next question.

"I know what the Emperor plans to do. I may have been cruel to you but that doesn't mean I have no care for the human race. Once he takes over, I don't believe he will stop. I understand how he plans to do it, and I believe we can stop him. We have to find the Amethyst Idol."

Aila

This was the first I'd heard of the Amethyst Idol, so I listened closely.

"The Amethyst Idol is a myth," Dorin said.

"No. It exists, and it is the Emperor's map to success. He's hidden it somewhere until he can use it. The date it will be unlocked is February 2, 2020. We have seven years to find it. I was there after another witch deciphered its codes. The Emperor had me banish her and Drake Ryan to the central world three years ago. Then, I overheard him talking to your brother. He has given it to someone he trusts for safekeeping. Your brother has plans of his own. He wants to become the leader of the council," Tallia explained.

"We can talk about finding the Idol later, right now we have to figure out a plan. How many are coming?" Dorin asked.

"A small army, including drudges. My guess is five guardians and seven to ten drudges," Bill said. "Heath and Andrei might show up too. Or, at least, Andrei. They want to keep the operation quiet. Heath doesn't want to reveal his plan quite yet."

"Great. That's three vampires and a witch against fifteen obsidian-bearing men. We can't put Aila's family at risk. We need to get them out of here and kill off anyone who dares threaten us," Dorin said.

"I agree, but we need obsidian," I replied.

"We brought some," Bill said as he handed a dagger to each of us.

"I wish I could have gotten more, but I have three bloodstones. One for each of you," said Tallia.

"What's this for?" I asked as I held the green and red speckled stone.

"It will protect you from one obsidian dagger to the heart. After you have been stabbed once, it will not work a second time," Tallia said.

"Thank you," I replied.

Bill and Dorin each took a bloodstone and started scouting for places to lead the drudges and guardians to. I decided to stay at the cabin to keep an eye on things. We agreed to wake my parents and friends in a few hours so they could get some sleep before going on the run again.

Tallia and I stood outside watching for any signs of intruders. It was generally silent in the cool night air. The sky was illuminated with Northern Lights.

"The moonstone seems to have had an effect on your senses, I see," Tallia said.

"Yes. It seems like every day I'm more and more aware of my surroundings."

"I noticed that you knew we were here before Dorin did. That's something. What else have you developed?"

"I'm able to see through walls and read minds," I said. "I also learned to control the mind reading. I can turn it off and on like a light switch."

"That has been rumored to take place around the age of six hundred. It's quite an amazing gift. I'm glad you were the one I gave it to. You seem to be very graceful about it. I know you will not abuse your abilities," Tallia said.

I smiled. "I'm very grateful for what you did for me. I need to ask you something, though. Did you know Dorin and I would find each other all those years ago when you cursed him?"

"I knew there would be a woman. I did not know your name, but I knew he would meet a woman that had the ability to give him back his humanity. That's all I ever wanted for him. Andrei was too far gone to be helped. I had no idea what he would try to do in his fit of jealousy. I am sorry for what he did to you."

"It's not your fault, Tallia. He's an evil man. I think Dorin will kill him someday. Maybe tomorrow if he gets the chance. Andrei has chosen to remain against us."

"Now that the curse is broken, if he openly tries to destroy either of you, he will turn to stone. I'm sure he knows that, so you must be careful to keep him away from your friends and family," Tallia said.

I nodded. He wouldn't get anywhere near them.

CHAPTER THIRTY-SIX

Dorin

"Who would have guessed everything would lead up to this?" Bill asked as we scouted the area.

"How do you mean?" I asked.

"Well, back when you first hired me, you advised that my back seat might get a little—bloody. Now Aila's a vampire. Heck a better vampire than either of us, now. She sensed Tallia and I before you did."

I chuckled. "I too was impressed by that."

"We're rogue now and I'm a shifter. I just wouldn't have guessed that taking a chauffeur job would have changed so much."

"You're right. Everything has led to this. Now nothing's more important than putting an end to Heath's reign."

We stumbled into a clearing. I looked around and then up at the night sky.

"I think this will do," I said to Bill. He nodded in agreement.

Aila

Dorin and Bill returned to the cabin. They seemed to have a plan. I could hear Dorin's thoughts. His plan was to lead them to a clearing about a mile south while I got my family to the plane. Tallia would go with me, but Bill and Dorin would lead the small army away from us.

"Do you think it will work? Isn't it me they're after?" I asked.

"Yes, but they'll think you're with me. They also want Bill since he's a shifter. They will most likely split up. Hopefully, most will follow us. It will be easier to handle them in small groups."

"Tallia, how long until they arrive?" Bill asked.

Tallia closed her eyes and dug a stone from her pocket. She held it close to her heart for a few moments. When she opened them again she said, "They will be here by eleven a.m."

"We should wake up the adults," I said.

"Yes. It's almost five," Dorin replied.

I went inside and woke my parents first and then Carmen and Steve. Little Collin slept as though nothing was going on, and that's how Carmen wanted it. Carmen packed hers and Steve's belongings.

"So, where are we going again?" she asked.

"We're going to Romania. Dorin has a place in the Carpathians that not even his evil brother knows about. He says it will be the safest place. It was his first choice originally, but going overseas is harder than just going from the U.S. to Canada. Dorin has a lot more connections and now that he's had time to contact them, we're all set," I explained.

"Won't it be sort of a culture shock? I mean, Romania is much different than Canada."

"Yes, but our safety is more important. Besides, the Emperor doesn't know Romania. He has no idea how many vampires are on Dorin's side. Since Andrei spent his time in the U.S. neither does he. Andrei cut off all connections to Romania a long time ago, so he won't know who to trust."

"How does this all work? We need to go to Yellowknife, right?"

"Right and we're taking two separate planes. Dorin and Bill are staying behind while Tallia and I get you all to the plane we took here. If we get there safely, and I sense that they need my help, Tallia will accompany you to Romania and I'll stay behind and help Dorin and Bill. We'll be right behind you. Tallia is trustworthy. She's the reason I don't need to drink human blood."

"Alright, but I hope you can come with us. I hope Dorin and Bill will get out of here quickly, too."

"If we want to get to Yellowknife by eleven we have to leave by seven. The roads might be bad today. Plus we want to get there as soon as possible to avoid run-ins with the Emperor and his minions."

"Right. We'll be ready by six-thirty," Carmen said.

I left the room to talk to my parents. They were busy packing their own things. My mother packed clothing and supplies and my father packed guns and defense weapons. My mother was almost cheerful about visiting a new country while dad was all business and in a military state of mind.

"We should leave by seven at the latest. Carmen said they'd be ready by six-thirty," I announced.

"That's fine, dear. I'm sure we'll be ready by six-thirty as well."

"Did Dorin explain all the details?" I asked.

"Yes, he did. He seems to have things squared away pretty well. We haven't met Tallia yet, but I understand she's to accompany us with or without you?" my father asked.

"Yes. She's very trustworthy. You'll like her. She's the reason I don't need to drink human blood." I repeated the same reassurance I'd use with Carmen.

"When can we meet her?" Kitty asked.

"I'll go find her right now," I replied.

I returned with Tallia in tow and made the introductions. My dad held out his hand for her to shake it and held up a gun.

"Ever used one of these?"

"I have, but I don't like to. I have other ways of protecting our group if it comes to that. I'm sure Aila told you a little about me?"

"Yes, she told us you were a witch. Is that right?" my mother asked.

"Yes, and I'm fairly powerful for my race. I've been around for over a hundred years, and I'd like to keep it that way as well as keep you all safe. If it makes you feel better, I'll carry a gun, but I promise I won't need it."

"Well—just to be safe," my dad said, handing a pistol and ammo to her.

"Got one of those for me?" asked Steve as he walked into the room.

"Sure do," he replied, handing him a rifle and handgun. I introduced Tallia and Steve before leaving the room to find Dorin.

CHAPTER THIRTY-SEVEN

Dorin

I stood watch just outside the main doors to the cabin. Bill was on a property run. And Tallia had isolated herself so she could keep a magical tab on Heath and the others. She wanted to make sure plans didn't change. Aila stepped out of the cabin and leaned against the other side of the main doors across from me. I admired the way she carried herself when she was in this alert state of mind. Her eyes roamed over the landscape with quick, yet thorough efficiency—possibly even seeing things I couldn't.

The orange glow of the morning sun illuminated her face. I smiled and turned to the south to check for any oncoming vehicles.

Aila approached me from behind, and gently put her hands on my shoulders before rubbing them across my back and then coming to stand next to me.

The cool air felt refreshing, but rain was coming.

"I think everything is going okay. I introduced Tallia to everyone," Aila said.

"That's good," I replied as I turned to face her. I put my arms around her and pulled her close. "We'll get everyone out safe, I promise."

Aila sunk into my embrace. I rested my chin on her head and wished we were already in Romania, curled up in my mountain home. I was anxious to leave Canada, even though it had provided beautiful views of the Northern Lights and amazing scenery. I wanted to be in my own territory.

Aila

"I should be able to tap into your thoughts from Yellowknife. I know your mind better than Bill's so I'll be able to keep track of what's going on. So don't think anything embarrassing," I teased.

"I'll try not to. What about the kind of thoughts I'm having right now? Are those allowed?"

I listened in to his beautiful mind. He thought about making love to me. Adrenaline surged through me for a split second.

I shook my head. "Save that for when everyone is safe and sound. I don't want you getting distracted, although it's intriguing to see how you picture our next time to be."

He smirked.

"Alright. Head in the game—got it," he said before pulling me in for a kiss.

Soon it was time for us to part ways. Tallia, Steve, Carmen, Collin, and my parents all piled into the SUV. I decided to run outside the vehicle and slightly ahead so I could sense any coming danger.

It would be a long run and I was glad I drank my fill the night before. The road ahead was clear for the time being. I'd recognize the thoughts of someone that was after us from miles away. Tallia drove the car. I listened in on her thoughts too, in case someone approached from behind.

About halfway to Yellowknife, I heard something. At first, it was faint and I could barely make it out, but it soon became clear I was hearing Andrei's thoughts.

. . . *see my brother among all those humans. It's a wonder he hasn't killed them all himself. I don't have that kind of self-control. Seeing Aila again will certainly be interesting. It's too bad she has to be killed too, with her powers developing at an accelerated rate, she could be useful. It's possible she's developed more than the x-ray vision trick. What was it that is supposed to come after that?*

I found the vehicle that carried Andrei and four others two miles ahead of the vehicle my family traveled in. I used all my strength to crash into the vehicle and overturn it before Andrei, the two other vampires, and the two drudges even knew I was in range. The SUV lay on its side in the ditch. The two drudges had either been killed in the tumbling crash or were unconscious.

Andrei was the first to emerge from the steaming wreck. I smiled.

"It's a pity you can't do anything to get me back for that."

"What are you talking about?" Andrei asked.

"The curse? If you openly try to destroy Dorin or me you'll turn to stone."

"I guess these boys will have to do my dirty work then," he replied as the other two vampires emerged.

They quickly reached me with obsidian daggers in their hands, but I could hear their thoughts, and, therefore, avoided every move they made at my heart. I was surprised at how easily it came to me.

Eventually, I used my own dagger to kill one of them. I witnessed for the first time with my superior eyes, what would happen to me if anyone ever succeeded in killing me. The vampire's body shriveled into a black ball of nothing right in front of me. I gasped but had little time to gawk.

By this time, Tallia and the others neared the scene in the SUV. I needed to kill the other one before they arrived so I'd only have Andrei to worry about. As the second vampire used his quick speed to lunge at me, I avoided the hit just in time, only to stake him in the heart with my dagger. His body shriveled just like the other. I collected the daggers of the two dead vampires.

"Very impressive," Andrei said, "Dorin must have been training you."

"Nope," I said, circling him like a shark. I could kill him, but any attempt on my life by him would result in him turning to stone.

"I just have a sense for what others will do next," I said.

"That's right, I remember now. The next power to develop is mind reading. Heath will be happy to be informed of this," Andrei said.

I cursed myself. The comeback should've stayed in the vault.

"Don't think I'll let you slip between my fingers so easily. You have a debt to me for what you did back in Florida."

"You can try to kill me, but I have enough bloodstone on me to supply an army," Andrei said, as he turned his attention to the approaching SUV. I took advantage of his distraction and tackled him, pushing him into the forest so Tallia could get through.

"You're going to have to do better than that," Andrei shouted as he recovered and ran with lightning speed toward the road and the SUV carrying my loved ones. I intercepted him and stopped him from reaching the SUV again. This time, I tumbled into the trees with him. I stabbed him in the arm with my dagger. He'd be injured and bloodstone only protected from blows to the heart.

Andrei's groan was a welcome sound as I pulled the dagger from his arm and watched as it went lifeless to his side. He'd heal, but it would take a while. I took a stab at the other arm as he tried to cradle the first. He blocked it and sent a punch flying into the air. It almost connected with my face, but his thoughts warned me of the attack.

Anger rocked through me and I tackled him again. I was ready to throw a punch myself, but Andrei pushed me off. I was flung across the small clearing and into a tree.

Andrei stood and yelled, "This won't be the last time you see me. Mark my words, you will not get the happiness you and Dorin think you're entitled to."

With that, he ran off in the opposite direction of my family with thoughts of the Emperor in his head accompanied by thoughts of revenge.

I decided it would be best not to follow him. I wanted to get my family onto the plane, safe and sound, before I worried about where he was going. I caught up to the SUV in no time and sensed no danger for the rest of the trip. Soon, we made it to the airport without incident.

My connection with Dorin told me that he and Bill were doing okay with the troop that arrived at the cabin, but I decided to stay behind anyway since Andrei was still in the area.

"I have to hunt him down," I told my family. "He knows I can read minds, and it's best that he doesn't relay the information to the Emperor. You'll be safe with Tallia."

We said our goodbyes and I watched as the plane took off. I'd see them soon in Romania.

Once I was sure the plane took off safely, I ran back toward the cabin. Andrei was just on the edge of my mind reading range and I caught small thoughts now and then. He was heading toward Dorin and Bill, and so was the Emperor.

The Emperor's thoughts started coming to me soon after, and once I was in range of Andrei and the Emperor I could see they meant business. They were there to kill Dorin, Bill, and me. Unfortunately, the Emperor could only be killed with emerald and obsidian. We had obsidian, but no emerald large enough to kill him.

I reached Dorin and Bill just as they finished off the last of the vampires and drudges from the Empire. Andrei was circling the clearing from far away, waiting until the Emperor arrived to make his move.

"Andrei's here and he's injured," I reported, "The Emperor is near too, and they're planning on confronting us together."

Dorin nodded and we all stood in the clearing, ready for them to show their faces.

"They found each other and are on their way here. Two minutes," I said. Unfortunately, Andrei already told the Emperor about my gift. Two minutes later, the two spawns of evil came strolling into the clearing.

"Dorin, Aila, and Bill. Didn't think I'd see you here, Bill," Heath said. It was a lie. He knew Bill was here before he even got on the plane.

"Andrei just told me some interesting news. Something I'd suspected, but not something I'd yet confirmed. Aila, you developed a new power. Such a pity you decided to run instead of joining us in our quest."

"I still retain my humanity, something you haven't had in a long time," I replied.

"Humanity is overrated. Dorin, I thought you would see things my way. We were so close during the war. It's too bad you aren't more like your brother. He is loyal."

"Loyalty means nothing when you're talking about enslaving the human race," Dorin said.

"Another annoyance is that you've taken care of all the troops I sent in before me. Andrei is useless to me right now as it seems Aila's gift has enabled her to wound him. It's hard to believe you'd do this to someone who can't fight back."

"He did much the same to me, and he knows it," I replied with a glare in Andrei's direction.

"Well then, the score should be settled," Heath said.

"I'll say when the score is settled," I said.

Heath sighed and looked toward Andrei. "It seems we're at a draw, considering I'm much too outnumbered to actually be able to kill any of you. Andrei won't be much help, thanks to Aila. Seeing as you have no emerald to kill me with—let's call it a day. Just remember that we will hunt you down. We'll find your family too, Aila. Tallia should also watch her back if she knows what's good for her. Don't think you can stop us. Not even I know the location of the Amethyst Idol, so you'll have to come up with another plan, Aila."

I glared at the Emperor, but he told the truth. As far as I could tell, the second he suspected I could read minds, he activated a chain of command and a vampire somewhere along that chain would have it. Names flowed into my head and mixed together like ingredients in a stew. Deciphering them would be impossible and finding the one that actually had it would be out of the question.

"It's too bad you had to take the road of the rebel, Dorin. You'd be so useful—and Aila too. Bill, I hope you got what you needed from your mentor because you have a long way to go before you can keep up with him. Au revoir, for now," Heath said before disappearing with Andrei into the woods.

I tracked his thoughts for a while longer to make sure they were actually leaving. Once I was certain, I told Bill and Dorin it was safe to leave.

CHAPTER THIRTY-EIGHT

Dorin

The second plane I chartered was much like my own private jet. After the long flight, broken up by two stops, we finally arrived in Romania. Aila's family had stayed at a hotel with Tallia as their tour guide and it was the morning after the confrontation with Heath and Andrei.

I bought two vehicles suitable for off-roading for the group to travel in and we headed from Bucharest into the mountains to find my home.

Eight hours later, we came to a stop. I had been driving one of the SUV's to lead the way. Aila was at my side. The other car pulled up next to us and I rolled down the window to communicate with them.

"We have to go up that trail, and then it's about a half-hour hike to get to my place."

I could hear the groans of the other travelers. They were all tired and ready for bed. The sun was sinking in the sky and the mountain glowed in the rays of the sunset. I noted the beautiful contrast of green and gray. I was about to point it out to everyone, but they were too tired to care.

"I promise it will be worth it," I said to the other car before rolling my window back up and starting up the bumpy trail. After a while, we came to a clearing where I parked the SUV and gestured for Tallia to do the same with the other. Bill, Aila and I volunteered to carry most of the gear.

Everyone was happy to stretch their legs, but still unsure of walking for half an hour. Little Collin was tired, and Steve and Carmen took turns carrying him.

Finally, I lead everyone toward a cave entrance.

"I thought you had a house up here," Steve asked.

"I do, although it's not a house in the traditional sense, but I'm sure you won't be disappointed," I replied, as I lit a torch and led the way into the cave. Inside, it looked like an ordinary cave. After a few twists and turns, I stopped at what looked like a dead end, but I knew better.

"Want to help me with this, Bill?" I asked.

"Sure thing," Bill said as he stepped toward the dead end. I instructed Bill to take hold of one side of the large boulder while I took the other. We moved the massive thing aside to reveal a wooden door.

I took out my keys and unlocked the door before flipping a switch on the outside.

"Give it a moment," I said.

The sound of electricity coursing through wires came to my ears, just before the inside of the room I opened illuminated.

"Home, sweet home," I said, gesturing for everyone to enter.

Aila's family cautiously stepped inside. The room inside the cave was a large cavern, but nicely carved and smoothed to look like a large, stone living room. Luxurious furniture decorated the inside. Two couches, a few recliners, and even an entertainment center complete with a TV and stereo system.

Drapery on the walls and rugs on the floor made it seem even cozier.

"So, this is the living room," I said, closing the door once everyone stepped inside. "Down that hallway is the kitchen and dining room, and down the other you'll find the bedrooms."

"How did this get here?" Brian asked.

"I put it here," I said. "I had a lot of time on my hands before I came to the United States. I wanted a place where I could start my own sort of family if I ever wanted to. Now, the bathrooms have one problem—no toilet, but I can fix that over the next few weeks. There's a small supply of running water. We'll have to replenish it occasionally. For now, I'm afraid we'll have to make some kind of area just outside for you humans to, uh, have human time."

"This is amazing," Aila said, "I can't believe you did all this on your own."

"Well, I had some help from Tavian. I wish he could be here with us." I said with a twinge of sadness.

"I hope this place suits everyone," I said, turning to the awestruck group of humans.

"This place is wonderful Dorin," Kitty said, "It will do just fine for us."

"I think it will work as long as we've got a bedroom and, at some point, a bed for Collin," Carmen said.

"Yes, of course. Bill and I can go to the nearest town for supplies and anything you all might need or want to make it seem more comfortable. The bedrooms have small windows that overlook the valley. Curtains cover those windows during the night so no one can see the light from your rooms. You're welcome to let in sunshine and air during the day, of course."

Kitty and Brian settled into a room and Carmen, Steve, and Collin found another that would suit them. Each bedroom had a king sized bed and plenty of furnishings to make it feel like home. Tallia and Bill each had a room to themselves as well.

Aila and I took the master bedroom I carved out for myself. The room was different from the others. The walls had beautiful ornate designs carved into them, and I hand-picked the furniture to go with the designs. It had a bathroom with a tub, shower, and sink. The tub and sink were carved from stone and coated with a protective barrier.

"This is wonderful," Aila said.

I looked into her eyes from across the room and was at her side in a blink of an eye. "I hoped you would like it. Of course, this is your home too. We can change anything you want."

"I don't want to change a thing. It's all so grand, yet natural and welcoming. I love it."

"Good," I said before giving her a kiss.

"What's next on the agenda? I mean where do we go from here?"

"Well, I thought we'd take a little break from all the serious stuff and plan a wedding."

"I would like nothing more, but what about the Emperor?"

"That can wait. We have a long time before his plan goes into action and I don't think he'll find us here for a while. I think what we all need right now is a little happiness and a little normalcy."

"Okay, so when do you want to get married?"

"I was thinking we could get married on my mothers' birthday."

"Okay, and when is that?" Aila asked.

"In about a month. Think we can handle it?"

Aila laughed. "I don't have to sleep anymore. Anything is possible. Besides, it's just going to be a small wedding for everyone here, right?"

"If that's what you want."

"It is. They are the people who matter the most to us," Aila replied.

I kissed her. Then we relaxed on the bed and began to make new plans for our wedding.

Aila

A month later, on the 5th day of July, I wore my wedding dress. Carmen and my mother were doing my hair. That is, Carmen was doing my hair and my mother was tearing up every time she looked at me.

"Mom, please stop crying. You're making me want to cry, but I can't."

"I know, but you just look so beautiful!" she said.

"Thank you, mom. You do too. Do you like the dress Dorin bought for you?"

"Oh, yes. It's beautiful. He's so generous. He's going to make you so happy and I know you make him happy too."

"I hope we have the same wonderful kind of marriage you and dad have," I replied.

"Yours will be even better. It will stand the test of time. Ours will stand the test of a lifetime."

"Oh, mom. Yours will stand the test of time too. I will never forget the way you and dad work so well together. And Carmen, you and Steve are an inspiration too. You found true love, and so did we. We are three very happy girls, with three wonderful men."

Carmen smiled and gave me a hug. "I'm all finished with your hair and makeup. We should be starting soon, are you ready?"

"It seems like I've been ready for a very long time," I replied.

My mother and Carmen gave me one more hug each before going to their seats. The wedding was just outside the mountain side home we'd all been living in. A clearing in the woods with a waterfall providing a soothing ambiance in the background was the perfect setting. Dorin had built a platform with a little canopy of white tulle for us to get married under. He brought in white chairs for the guests and a man who acted as a vampire justice of the peace. He was a vampire who catered to the rebel and loner vampires since he was a loner himself and had little to do with the dealings of the Empire.

Bill played music on an electric piano that set the romantic mood. Tallia was on the grooms' side and Bill would join her during the ceremony only a few feet from his piano. My mother, Carmen, Steve, and Collin sat on the brides' side with an empty chair for my father once he had given me away.

I took a deep breath, even though it was more of a habit than an actual need for oxygen. I stood, picked up my bouquet, and walked to the entrance of my brides' tent. Through the white canvas, I used my ability to see through walls to see Dorin standing at the end of the aisle, waiting for me. He was handsome in his suit. A smile, deep and true came to my face.

I couldn't be happier. Dorin was perfect, and my family had been so supportive.

I rang my bell, to signal that I was ready and Bill began the music. I stepped out of the tent and caught sight of Dorin's face when he saw me. I wished I could read his thoughts although I'd promised myself I wouldn't. I wanted the experience to be as human as possible, even though I slipped up with the x-ray vision. The look on his face would certainly suffice. The excitement and love in his eyes told me everything I needed to know. We'd be together forever, and nothing could come between us.

I walked down to meet my father and we went down the aisle together. My hand was in his and he handed it to Dorin once we reached the end. I kept myself from reading my father's thoughts as well, but I knew he was happy with my choice and that he approved wholeheartedly.

After that, my eyes never left Dorin's, and his never left mine.

We shared our first kiss as a married couple and walked back down the aisle while everyone clapped. A reception area was set up just down a short trail and we made our way to it, with everyone following behind.

Dancing, food and cake were planned, but just as we entered the reception area, I caught wind of a random thought in the voice of the Emperor.

Then, another in Andrei's voice.

I stopped dead in my tracks.

"Get everyone to the helicopter," I said, turning and walking back to my family.

"They're here?" Dorin asked.

"Yes. They will be in about ten minutes."

Bill's vampire hearing had caught the entire conversation and he ran to the helicopter to get it ready for takeoff.

My parents could tell something was wrong, soon Carmen and Steve caught on too.

"Get to the helicopter. Bill will take you where it's safe," I said to them.

"What about you guys?" my father asked.

"We'll be fine. We have an emerald if the Emperor tries anything," Dorin said. "Don't be afraid to use those guns in the helicopter if you need to."

"Never been afraid to use a gun in my life, son," my father said.

"We'll see you at the rendezvous," I said as we parted ways. Bill would go with them and protect them. Tallia stayed behind with us.

"It's a good thing our piano player is also a helicopter pilot," Dorin said.

"Don't forget he can pilot a yacht, too," I replied.

Five minutes later, the helicopter was loaded with passengers and emergency cargo and ready for takeoff. Bill signaled to us before taking off. I watched for a second time as my family avoided destruction. I was getting sick of Andrei and the Emperor ruining our peace. They would not get away unscathed if I had anything to do with it.

The minutes stretched on, finally Andrei and the Emperor, along with a few drudges and newborn vampires for protection, came into the clearing where Dorin and I were supposed to be celebrating our marriage.

CHAPTER THIRTY-NINE

Dorin

"You guys didn't have to dress up for us," Heath commented with a smirk.

"You just missed our wedding, but you'll pay for ruining our reception," Aila replied.

"I'm so disappointed that we weren't invited. Looks like it was a beautiful ceremony. Too bad the marriage won't last long. I'm afraid "'til death do you part" will come sooner than you expected," Heath said.

"We've prepared this time," I said, brandishing a sharp piece of emerald and an obsidian dagger. The Emperor eyed them with caution.

"So have we," Andrei said gesturing for the drudges and newborn vampires to step forward.

"You think those scare us?" Aila asked with a chuckle, brandishing her own obsidian dagger and a gun she hid under her wedding dress. She was sexy when she bantered.

Tallia revealed her dagger as well. She didn't need a gun to deal with the humans.

"We thought they might slow you down a little," Andrei replied.

"I wonder," Aila began, "if any of you have ever seen a vampire fly?" Aila's body then lifted off the ground. She hovered above Tallia and I. The looks on the faces of our enemies said they hadn't prepared for Aila's new ability. She discovered it only a few weeks prior, but gained control of it.

I grinned with glee as my beautiful new wife intimidated the hell out of all of them—including the Emperor.

Aila

The thoughts of the drudges and newborns ranged from *Oh, shit!* to *So, what?*

I decided to go for the ones who doubted my ability first. I shot at one of the drudges and flew toward a young vampire with my dagger. The bullet hit the arm of a drudge and I successfully plunged the dagger into the heart of the vampire, who shriveled into nothing.

"What? You didn't want to waste bloodstone on them?" I asked.

Dorin attacked a vampire with his own dagger, and after a brief struggle, ended his life.

Tallia used her magic to disable the drudges' guns. Once they found out they could no longer use them, they took out their own obsidian daggers.

I read the drudges' minds. They were starting to think they were in over their heads.

"Wondering what you're doing here? Wondering how you can possibly defeat us?" I asked. "I'll tell you one thing. You're only here to distract us and provide a barrier between us and the Emperor. You are mere pawns."

I lowered myself to the ground.

"If you think they care about whether you live or die, I can tell you right now that they don't."

The drudges were starting to look to one another for reassurance, but none could find it. Tallia was working on some sort of chant. The drudges were frozen in time.

I glanced to Tallia.

"I want to spare them if possible, but we need to take care of the vampires first," Tallia explained.

I nodded and focused my attention on a vampire with bright green eyes. Another sprinted at Tallia, but she wore a protective ring, and he bounced off the invisible shield it produced.

Dorin had his eye on the third and final newborn.

I leaped into the air and crashed into the vampire I squared off with. This one had a dagger and he wasn't afraid to use it.

Dorin's thoughts became distracted at my struggle with the vampire, and the third vampire crashed into him. His thoughts were also distracting me as my enemy landed a punch to my stomach. I momentarily stalled but recovered in time to block another attempt.

I was jabbing with my dagger and blocking blows at the same time. I had to separate myself from Dorin's thoughts to focus on the other vampires. Once I did, I found it easy to see exactly what he was going to do next, and finally ended him. My ability instantly turned back to Dorin's thoughts, he was doing just fine. He had the upper hand, but of course, he fought in the Great Vampire War and survived. He could obviously take on a newborn vampire.

Eventually, Dorin killed the other vampire and Tallia killed hers.

The only beings standing in the clearing were four frozen drudges, four powerful vampires, and one powerful witch. The Emperor came forward with Andrei, stepping around the frozen drudges. We readied ourselves.

"Impressive," the Emperor said. "I forgot how well you fought in the war. Perhaps you forgot how well I fought in the war too?"

"I haven't forgotten," Dorin said. "In fact, I was counting on it."

"Now, Tallia. Why don't you allow Andrei to defend himself?" the Emperor asked.

"Andrei should sit this one out," Tallia replied.

"That's too bad. I guess I'll have to call on my own secret weapon. Sarah?"

From the woods, a woman emerged. She was beautiful with blue eyes, blond hair, and fair skin. I knew instantly that she was also a witch. One thing I didn't know was what she was thinking.

"I can't read her," I said. "She must be able to block me."

"Yes, she's blocking you, I can see it now. I should have known," Tallia replied.

"Sarah, would you do the honors and give Andrei the ability to protect himself from Aila?"

Sarah nodded at the Emperor and cast her spell. A pulse of energy burst out from Andrei the instant she broke Tallia's spell.

Tallia glared at her. "You were never on my side. I should have known you'd do what no other witch would do. After all you've done, I shouldn't be surprised that you're here."

"You're one to talk about ethics," Sarah replied in a hateful voice, "Look what you've done to these two brothers. You tore them apart."

"I'll tear you apart!" Tallia yelled back. "It's not like you're all that innocent either. At least I made it right with my victims—or at least, tried to." Tallia shot a glance at Andrei.

Then she added, "If I ever meet him, I'll take your curse from him. I know he still walks the earth. You made sure of that."

"Only during the day," Sarah smirked. "The rest of the time he's pretty still. Besides, he broke my heart. These men broke yours. I thought you'd be happy. You saved one of them, and I saved the other," Sarah replied.

With that, Tallia whipped up a cloud of white magic energy and hurled it towards Sarah. Sarah stopped it with her own black cloud.

I took Andrei's distraction as a time of opportunity and I crashed into him as Dorin and Heath collided at the same time.

Andrei's thoughts were wild and I was having a hard time keeping up. I again forced myself to forget about Dorin and Tallia's thoughts and focus on Andrei's.

He was well trained, like Dorin and Heath, but I had a few advantages. As Andrei came at my chest with a dagger, I jumped into the air. I flipped around and used my own dagger. He moved just in time and I only sliced his ribcage. I knew he had bloodstone on him. Two, to be exact. I only held one dagger, so I hoped Tallia could beat Sarah and Andrei would turn to stone.

As for the Emperor, I wasn't sure how to kill him. He had three bloodstones, which meant we'd have to pierce his heart with four daggers. We only had three which meant we needed the Emperor's or Andrei's dagger to kill him.

The whole fight hinged on whether or not Tallia could over power Sarah. I floated into the air to get away from Andrei long enough to see how Tallia was progressing, and to see how Dorin was doing with Heath.

Tallia and Sarah were locked in a battle of translucent shields and forces of energy. The white cloud created by Tallia started to overpower the black cloud created by Sarah. I wondered for a moment who Sarah cursed years ago—the man that Tallia scolded her for and vowed to help. If only I knew, maybe I could distract Sarah long enough for Tallia to get the upper hand.

I turned my attention to Heath and Dorin who were locked in a fierce battle. Obsidian was flying through the air in the hands of two skilled, ancient vampires.

Dorin had a few slices and scratches, and Heath did too. It seemed that Heath's royal status meant he healed a little faster.

With my mind distracted, I lost track of Andrei, but my quick senses alerted me to his attack. He'd climbed a tree and was now hurtling toward me at full force. I blocked the dagger, and instead of it landing in my chest, it pierced the skin and muscle just below the shoulder. Pain spiked through me as I tumbled to the ground with Andrei right on top of me.

Recovering, I pulled the dagger out of my shoulder and bared my fangs at Andrei who was a few feet away, standing up from the hard landing and brushing the dirt off his clothes. I now had two daggers. Exactly enough to kill the Emperor. I looked to Tallia as Andrei and I circled each other. He was going to try to get his dagger back, but I wouldn't let that happen.

I searched Tallia's mind to find information on the man who broke Sarah's heart. Finally, I found it. Sarah had been in love with a man named Jesse Sutton. They were to marry in the 1920's, but he did not love her. She found out about another woman he was seeing on the side and cursed him. Since he snuck around with the woman at night, he was cursed to never walk at night again. He would turn to stone between sunset and sunrise and be forced to live this way for an eternity.

I knew the story, so I just had to figure out how to distract Sarah with the information.

First I'd have to get Andrei off my back for a moment. I turned my gaze on him and glared, then ran full force at him and hit him with such force that he went far into the woods. I regained my stature and turned toward Sarah.

"So you're the witch who plays dirty?" I asked.

Sarah's gaze turned to me for a quick moment but instantly went back to Tallia.

"Maybe that's why he didn't love you. You're cruel and he couldn't take it. He didn't want to hurt your feelings. That's why he snuck around with another woman."

Tallia's white magic forced itself closer to Sarah as she lost her composure. Tallia's mind fed me more information.

Sarah had also been the reason Heath was able to kill the previous Emperor. Sarah loved Heath too, but he would never be with her.

"Now you try to help Heath again. Unfortunately, he's still dedicated to his wife. You know if you try to hurt Iris he'll have you banished. You're so pathetic. He doesn't give a damn about you. He's only using you for your powers."

Andrei recovered at this point and was running at me full force, but it was too late. Tallia's magic won out and she replaced her spell. Andrei's pace began to slow as his body stiffened up and turned to stone.

Sarah let out a shriek and attempted to blast Tallia with her magic, but her magic had been drained. When it didn't work, she used what little magic she had left to disappear into thin air. The Emperor was now outnumbered.

Dorin was cut and wounded. The Emperor was too. Neither of them landed a dagger in the heart, although it looked as if they came close. My shoulder hurt and my arm was heavy with the usually insignificant weight of the dagger. I still carried one in each hand as Tallia and I approached the battle of the two vampires.

The Emperor seemed to notice he was losing. Thoughts in his mind came in quick succession. He knew the only chance he had was to get rid of two of the daggers. I could see his plan form, but my wound prevented me from reacting fast enough. He dove into Dorin at the opportune moment. They each landed their dagger in the other's heart. The effects of the bloodstone melted the daggers away before they could do any damage.

I instantly ran to Dorin as the Emperor backed off. Tallia kept her eye on him.

"Are you alright?" I asked, helping him to his feet.

"I'm fine," Dorin said. He took one of the daggers that I held and started to walk back toward the Emperor. Then, the second part of Heath's plan revealed itself to me. With lightning speed, the Emperor took the dagger from my hand and tossed me into a tree. He was heading straight for Dorin's heart, but Dorin was no longer protected by bloodstone. I was.

I flew into the air and landed in front of Dorin just before the dagger would have buried itself in his heart. Instead, the dagger pierced my chest. I felt the pain of the obsidian, but the bloodstone kept it from reaching my heart. The obsidian melted and flowed to the ground.

Much to the surprise of the Emperor, I'd taken the hit, and now Dorin and I were both alive, but unprotected. With the number of daggers down to two, it was another draw. We wouldn't be able to kill Heath, but we got rid of Andrei.

Sarah reappeared. She had tears in her eyes as she stood next to Heath.

"It seems we are again at a draw. I was hoping to kill you, Dorin. I guess you really do have the kind of love Iris and I share. Aila, you proved yourself worthy of the abilities you received, but that doesn't mean I won't be tracking you down once again. I won't stop until you are both dead. Sarah, take us home."

Sarah and the Emperor disappeared into thin air.

Tallia quickly tried to put a tracer on them with her magic, but she was too late. They were gone, and now that the Emperor knew we had an emerald big enough to kill him, he'd be in hiding.

I heard his thoughts, but they hadn't revealed the location of his hideout or the location of the Amethyst Idol.

"So, now what?" I asked as I turned to Dorin and Tallia.

"Now we search. There are only so many vampires the Emperor can trust with the Idol. It may take us a long time to find it, but we have to try," Dorin replied as he approached me and put his arm around me. His suit and my dress were both torn to shreds.

"Now that they have Sarah on their side, we will need to keep moving," Tallia said.

"Yes. I suppose it's a good thing I have my boat. We can use it to travel the world and search for the Idol. We have less than seven years before he puts his plan into action. He's waiting for technology to catch up. That will give us an opportunity to find the Idol and figure out how to destroy it."

"We can't destroy it," Tallia said.

"What? Why not?" Dorin asked.

"It holds a prophecy that must be fulfilled. If we find the Idol, we will find alliances and we will also find war. It's a war that I believe will end in our favor, but nonetheless, must be fought."

"So we can't stop them from taking over technology, but we can possibly stop them from taking over the world?" I asked.

"Yes. That's what I have come to believe."

"Seven years. I hope it doesn't take that long," I replied. "Let's get to the rendezvous so we can put my family at ease about our well-being. Not to mention we have to break the news that we'll be staying on the boat for an extended period of time."

Dorin hugged me, and Tallia cast her spell. The three of us surged through space to Dorin's yacht, where my family anxiously awaited our arrival.

NOTE FROM THE AUTHOR:

The following epilogue may contain spoilers for those who have not read book one, *Obsidian*.

EPILOGUE

SEVEN YEARS LATER . . .

Aila

I stood at the bow of the yacht as my group neared the Big Island of Hawaii. In our seven years of traveling the seas, we had yet to visit the Islands of Hawaii. We were getting close, I could feel it. We had missed the deadline to find the Idol before the Empire used it to transmit the virus, but we could still shut it down. The leads that we had been left with had all proved to be decoys. There were no other options. The Idol had to be in Hawaii.

Cruising up the east coast of the Big Island, I kept my eyes on the land. I longed for it. We had been at sea for days and I could no longer handle the boat. Cabin fever was no myth.

Collin, now seven years old, almost eight walked up to me.

"Aila, what's that?" he asked pointing to the distance.

I turned my head to see a tower of water fifty feet off the surface. At the top of the whirling water there seemed to be a woman. From this same point, it seemed as though balls of water were being shot at the cliff. I focused my vampire vision and realized the woman was actually throwing the water at the cliff—without using her hands or anything, really.

"Uh, go get Dorin, please Collin. I'm not sure what's going on but he might have an idea."

Collin happily ran off to fetch Dorin.

I kept an eye on the woman. I wondered if she was in trouble or perhaps she was trouble. Whoever she was, she seemed to be losing the angry energy she exuded. The balls of water started to shrink and less frequent.

Dorin was suddenly at my side.

"If I'm not mistaken, that is a siren," he said.

"Siren? They exist?"

"I thought they were extinct, but I must have been mistaken. No other being can do that."

I watched as the woman started to descend back to the surface.

"Let's go find out who she is," Dorin said, jumping into the water. I was right behind him. We swam with lightning speed to the place where the siren was now treading water.

As we neared, the siren caught sight of us and suddenly, her defenses were up. She drew large amounts of water into the air above her, ready to strike with great force. The woman before us was gorgeous. She had long dark hair and bright blue eyes that reminded me of my own.

"Whoa, we come in peace," Dorin said.

"You're vampires," the siren replied.

"Yes. We are vampires, but we don't want to hurt you. We just saw you from our boat over there. I thought sirens were extinct," Dorin replied.

The siren drew even more water into the growing mass of water that hovered above her. She obviously had reason not to trust vampires.

"Look," I said, "we just want to talk."

"If you think you're going to get my consent to change me, you are sorely mistaken. I'm no one's minion," the siren said with hatred.

Dorin and I looked at each other.

"You are referring to the fact that if a vampire changes you with your permission, that vampire will have power over you?" Dorin asked.

"Yes."

"That's not why we're here."

"Then why are you here?" the siren said coldly.

"We're looking for the vampires responsible for the virus," Dorin replied.

The siren seemed even more guarded with the mention of the virus. I couldn't help but think this siren knew something.

"We're trying to shut it down," I explained.

"How do I know Tom didn't send you?" the siren replied.

"We have people—humans—back on our boat. A witch too. They'll all tell you the same thing. Who's Tom?" Dorin asked.

I already knew. It was a name I'd seen in the Emperor's mind.

"Tom Walker?" I asked the siren. I tried using my ability to read minds on the siren, but I wasn't getting through.

"How did you know that?"

"It's complicated. We're trying to find the Amethyst Idol. If we destroy it, the virus will no longer exist. If you know anything, we'd be grateful for the information. We've been searching for it for seven years, ever since I learned of the Emperor's plan," I explained.

"Well, I don't know anything about an Amethyst Idol, but I do know Tom Walker is going to die. Hope he's not a friend of yours," she replied.

"We don't know him, but he might be the key to finding the Idol," Dorin replied.

"I wouldn't doubt it. He's behind everything around here. He's tried to turn me, he's tried to kill me and my friends on multiple occasions and he's succeeded in killing my parents and more recently, a person very dear to me." The siren looked toward the cliff.

She then turned back to us and continued. "I intend to make him pay for what he's done. If you're telling the truth, I can tell you exactly where to find him. He's the president of the Hawaii branch of Psytech. I'd say he's pretty connected in the vampire world. If the Amethyst Idol is on this or one of the other Hawaiian Islands, he knows about it."

"Why don't we converge and let our two groups meet?" Dorin asked, "Where are your friends?"

"We have a hidden spot over there, although our position has been compromised just today. It will be easier if I take you there," the siren said.

"I'm sure we can find it," Dorin replied.

"No, trust me. It will be much faster if we all swim back to your boat and I take you there," the siren replied.

Aila looked to Dorin who shrugged and started making his way back to the boat. The siren and I followed. She kept up with me easily as she used her powers to propel herself at high speed through the water. Once aboard, we introduced her to the others in our group. She was much more at ease once she met the humans. My father made his way toward the pilot house and asked where we were headed.

"Allow me," the siren said. Suddenly, the boat lurched toward the coast. It was moving quickly and quietly. For a second, I thought she was going to crash us into the cliff, but instead she guided us to a break in the cliff face.

The siren maneuvered the boat through a crevasse and into an open area shared with another boat. The occupants of my boat watched in amazement as we neared the other boat and came to a stop a short distance away.

The siren turned toward us and announced, "Welcome to our no-longer-secret cove. Let's meet the members of my group."

I looked at the siren in amazement. "I thought I was special. What's your name anyway?"

"Ava. Ava Tanner," the siren replied.

WHILE YOU WAIT FOR *AMETHYST* . . .

Fall into my other novel, *Where the Carnies Are*.

It's FREE for my VIP Readers. Just go to

kaylacurry.com/vip-reader-sign-up.

ABOUT THE AUTHOR

Kayla Curry's creative mind never sleeps. Literally.

At night, her active imagination produces dreams all night long. It's those dreams that provide much of the inspiration for her stories which have a little Victorian charm mixed with a fairy tale flair.

Her works include *Where the Carnies Are, Obsidian (Mystic Stones Series #1)*, and many short stories.

She lives in North Platte, Nebraska with her husband and two sons and she plans to keep writing and creating for the rest of her life.

ACKNOWLEDGEMENTS

Thank you to my wonderful editor, Samantha. I'm so happy to have you there to fix all my mistakes. You're the best.

Thanks to my family, friends, and ARC readers. Couldn't do this without you. I appreciate your support.

And a huge thank you to people who read and review books—especially indie books. I want each and every person who reads this book to know that I truly appreciate the time you give to reading in a world where time is at a premium.